ANNIHILATE ME
VOLUME I

A NOVEL BY

CHRISTINA ROSS

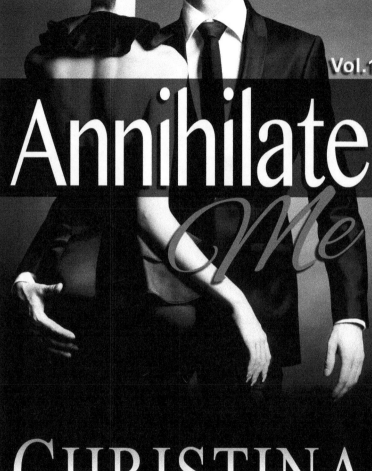

Vol.1

Annihilate *Me*

CHRISTINA ROSS

For Christopher, who knows why.

For Erika Rhys, in friendship.

For Ann Ross, for your love and support.

BOOK ONE

CHAPTER ONE

New York City
August

In my suffocating, one-bedroom, prison camp of an East Village apartment, I stood in front of the narrow mirror attached to my broken closet door and saw an older, messier version of myself staring back at me. I wondered who the hell was she—a distant relative, a long lost sibling, my ugly stepsister? All of the above? But then I was too distracted by the sweat coming through my white blouse to be sure or to even care.

What am I thinking? I look ridiculous. Not even ice in a freezer could keep cool in this heat. Call and cancel. Tell them there has been a death in the family—my hair.

"This isn't going to work," I called out. "My makeup is running down my face, my hair looks like a hot mess because of the humidity, and my clothes are starting to make the Hudson look dry. Why couldn't I have found a job in May or June? Or even July? I could be in a comfortable, air-conditioned office right now, doing my work, making light chit-chat with my elegant co-workers, laugh, laugh, laughing with them over the water cooler, and getting something I'll apparently never see in this city—a paycheck. But, oh no! For whatever reason, no one wants to hire me. So, today, I'll go and sit in front of some other prickly HR professional who will judge me to be unworthy and send me on my way."

I waited for a response, but none came.

I grabbed a magazine off my bed and started to fan myself with it. I walked to the doorway that entered into the living room, and found my best friend and roommate, Lisa Ward, typing at a quick clip on her MacBook Pro. She was nearing the end of her second novel, which she'd upload to Amazon in a few weeks. Given the success she enjoyed with her first book, which was an overall Top 100 best seller, I knew my time with Lisa might be brief if this book also took off. And I hoped it would, if only for her. Lisa had worked hard and she deserved it. At least one of us could enjoy our lives.

"You're awfully quiet," I said.

"That's because while you were in a full-on rant, I was taking notes. I'm going to use that mother of a tantrum for a scene in the new book. You were brilliant."

"You're putting me in your book?"

"I'm putting that rant in the book."

"Tell me I'll receive a royalty of some kind."

"How about dinner out? Like at a hot dog stand? We can afford that."

"Works for me. I'm Raman-noodled out."

Lisa pulled her blonde hair away from her face, wrapped it into a ponytail, and turned to look at me. Her skin was shiny from the heat, but even from where I stood, it appeared poreless. Lisa was one of those beautiful young women who could go without makeup and still look chic. She often said the same about me, though I never believed it. I'd never seen what others saw in me. I only wished I had Lisa's confidence.

"So, where is this interview?"

"At Wenn Enterprises."

"Never heard of it, but I'm not the business type. What's the job?"

"Oh, you'll love this."

"What?"

"I may have my master's degree in business— you know, the one that has sucker-punched me with forty thousand dollars' worth of debt—but because I'm essentially broke, I'm now going for a secretarial job."

"Jennifer—"

"It's fine. Wenn Enterprises is a successful conglomerate. Here's what I'm thinking. If I can get my foot in the door as a secretary, someone might see something in me, and in a few months, I'll have the job I've been seeking."

"I told you I'd give you money. The book is doing well, and this one is better than the first one, so maybe it'll do better."

"I appreciate that, Lisa. But I need to get out of this mess on my own. I still have a little left in savings. Enough to pay for next month's rent, but then I don't know what I'll do. If I don't get a job, I might have to go home."

"Why would you ever leave New York for Bangor, Maine? Why would you ever go back to your toxic parents? They just bring you down."

"The reality is that there is a bomb attached to my bank account, and it's about ready to explode. I've been frugal ever since we came here in May—no bars, no boys, no eating out, no new clothes, not even a latte—and it turns out I did the right thing. Otherwise, I would have been out of here at the end of June."

"You know," she said, "maybe you should consider a waitressing job at one of the city's better restaurants. You could clean up there at night, and then you could look for a job during the day. It wouldn't be easy, but if there's one thing I know about you, Jennifer, it's that you're tireless. The servers at some of the best restaurants make serious money. Six figures a year isn't uncommon here—and not many of them look as good as you do. Stop underestimating your looks. I think you're not getting a job because you intimidate the women who are interviewing you."

I overlooked the comment. I just didn't see in the mirror what others saw in me. Never had, never would. "I've actually thought about waitressing. And

I do have experience, though hardly at a high-end restaurant. Essentially, I shucked pizzas and beers to get through college."

Lisa held out her hands. "What you got at Pat's is experience. Whoever hires you will likely train you to serve their customers in the manner they expect anyway. Think about it. It would give you the money you need, and allow you to look for a job during the day. If this interview doesn't work out, that might be the magic bullet."

She was right. "Sorry I freaked out earlier."

"I'm not. That shit was good." Her face softened, and she looked at me with concern. "I just wish you weren't going through this. I know it's been difficult. I've seen how hard you've worked to find something. It'll happen at some point, but I'm as frustrated as you are that it hasn't happened yet. You deserve a good job."

"We're a team," I said. "Always have been."

"Since fifth grade."

"How's the book coming?"

"I'm actually digging it. The zombies are ferocious in this one. I think I might have the first draft done by the end of this week, and then it's all about the editing, which is good, because editing is the best part. You just slice and dice the words, reassemble them, read and re-read, get the book into its best possible shape, and put it out there."

"When can I read it?"

"The day it's finished. You're a great proofreader." Her eyes widened. "Hello. This town is filled with publishers. Have you considered that avenue?"

"I'm a business grad. They want English majors from Harvard."

"I wouldn't rule it out. You can do anything. I've always told you that."

"You're the best. I love you."

"I love you, too. It'll get better."

"I hope so. It's only the first week of August, and this is my seventh interview this month."

"Lucky seven. Now, go and take the hairdryer to yourself. Put it on cool, blot your face with a clean towel, and air yourself off. I'm giving you money for a cab, and I won't take no for an answer. Seriously. Don't even start with me. You need air conditioning. If this new book takes off, I'll buy us one for the apartment."

If this new book takes off, I'm afraid I'll lose you, which is another reason I have to find a job.

"OK," I said. "But you need to let me pay you back for the cab when I get a job."

"Fine. Whatever. Now, scoot. Your appointment is in ninety minutes. Traffic might be tight."

CHAPTER TWO

With my briefcase in hand, I left our sorry-looking apartment building on East Tenth Street, and stepped into the baking sun. Thankfully, at least, there was a breeze, which was rare these days. For the past month, Manhattan had been an airless sauna with the coals stacked high and some fool pouring ladles of water over them in a successful attempt to keep the air miserably moist.

I looked down the street for a cab, and, to my surprise, I didn't have to wait long to find one. I held out my hand, the driver spotted me, pulled toward the curb, and I stepped into the back seat, relieved to find that the air conditioning was turned to full blast. I positioned myself so the cool air flowed over me, and I took a breath. It felt wonderful.

"Fifth and Forty-Eighth," I said to the driver, an older woman with a shock of red hair that was clipped close. "The Wenn Enterprises building. Or as close as you can get me to it for twenty dollars."

The woman looked at me in the rearview mirror with a raised eyebrow. "I'll do my best. You know how it is during the lunch hour."

"Whatever you can do, I appreciate it. And please make sure you leave room for a tip. Unfortunately, five dollars is all I can afford."

"Don't worry about the tip," the woman said. "Some nice young man just gave me a twenty for a five-dollar fare. We'll take yours out of that."

I met the woman's eyes in the mirror. Sometimes, this city surprised me with its kindness. "Thank you."

"Just paying it forward, sweetie. Now, you do the same today. OK?"

"Deal."

And yet another reason why I love it here. Now, if I can just stay here. I've got to get this job.

We crossed over to Sixth Avenue, the driver hooked a left past the First Republic Bank and Jerri's Cleaners, and we started to move uptown. I kept my gaze fixed on the meter noticing how quickly we were burning through the money Lisa gave me when I left. Already, we were at eight dollars and counting. In this traffic, I'd be lucky if she got near Sixth and Fortieth Street, let alone Fifth and Fortieth.

And I was right. By the time we reached Thirty-Eighth Street, my twenty dollars was gone.

"This is fine," I said. "I can walk from here."

"You going back to work?"

"I wish I had work. I'm going for an interview. I think this is about my hundredth interview in the past few months."

"Looking like you do, I'd think someone would hire you in a minute."

Before I could deflect the compliment, the woman pressed a button. A receipt started to print, and she clicked off the meter. "Can't show up looking like a mop, now can you? No one's going to hire a mop. Don't worry about it. The fares uptown always pay. I'll make up for it."

"You're incredibly kind."

"Just paying it forward. I know what it's like trying to find a job in this rotten economy. Still pulling myself out of it. I take it you're not from here?"

"I'm from Maine. Moved here in May."

"Without a job?"

"Just one of the many stupid things I've done in my life. There's so much to offer here, I thought it would be easy to find work. Well, at least easier than finding work in Maine, where there are zero jobs."

"Nothing's easy in New York, sweetie. But pay it forward. Every day do someone a kindness. You'll see. Things will turn around for you. They did for me."

When we pulled alongside Wenn Enterprises, which was a gleaming, modern skyscraper that seemed to catch the sun and toss it back to kiss the sky, the woman adjusted her rearview mirror so I could look into it. "Do you have a compact?"

"I do," I said. I lowered my head and saw why she asked—despite the air conditioning, my face was shiny. I opened the right side of my bricfcasc and removed one.

"I'd blot."

"Blotting."

"Under the eyes."

"Eyes."

"Don't forget your neck."

"Neck."

"Now, kill the interview."

"You must have some very lucky children."

"I'm the lucky one," the woman said, taking the twenty I handed her. "I remind myself of that every day."

CHAPTER THREE

Once inside the lobby, which was a hive of activity as people stepped into and out of elevators and crisscrossed in front of me, I approached the reception area. I was so nervous that my heels sounded to me like drum taps on the marble floor.

A man looked up at me.

"I'm Jennifer Kent," I said. "I have an interview with Barbara Blackwell."

"Ms. Blackwell?"

"Sorry. Yes, Ms. Blackwell."

He typed something into his computer, read the screen, picked up the phone that was next to him, and made a call. "Jennifer Kent to see Ms. Blackwell.

Shall I send her up? I understand that she's early, but she's nevertheless here. Thank you."

He hung up the phone and motioned toward the elevators. "Fifty-first floor. Take a right when the doors open. You'll find a sitting area to your left. You're early. Wait there for a bit, and Ms. Blackwell's assistant will come for you."

"Thank you," I said. "Sorry I'm early."

"Better than late," he said.

* * *

When the doors opened, I steeled myself and stepped into the hallway. I saw the sitting area, went to it, and found it packed. There was no room to sit down. Fourteen faces looked up at me, eyes roamed over me, and one fat man stuffed into a gray business suit that barely contained his girth smiled suggestively at me.

"Excuse me," someone said as they brushed past me in the narrow hallway.

"Sorry."

"Right."

Christ.

"Julie Hopwood?"

I turned and saw a middle-aged woman standing next to me.

"No, I'm Jennifer—"

"I'm Julie Hopwood," a pretty brunette sitting next to the fat man said. She was polished and when she stood, I thought she looked smashing in her dark blue suit.

"You're here for the secretarial job?"

"I think we all are," she said.

The woman smiled tightly. "Right this way. Ms. Blackwell will see you now."

"Thank you."

As she moved past me, she said, "I've so got this."

Seriously?

I looked over at the fat man, who was staring at me, his lips slightly parted. *Why is he looking at me like I'm roast beef?* I certainly couldn't linger in the doorway, so I went over to the chair next to his and sat down. I put my briefcase in my lap, and noticed that his face was turned to mine. I didn't want to engage him, so I ignored him, snapped open my briefcase, and pretended to look inside for something until he finally looked away.

Fifteen minutes later, I caught sight of Julie Hopwood walking past the sitting room's door with a contented smile on her face. Then the older woman who had retrieved her a moment before asked for a Jennifer Kent.

"That's me," I said, standing.

"Ms. Blackwell will see you now."

"Thank you."

"Good luck," the fat man said.

I raised a hand in acknowledgement and continued toward the woman, who brought me down a long hallway to the open door of a corner office. Inside, I saw a severe-looking woman in a chic black business suit sitting at a large desk with the Manhattan skyline shining behind her in the sun. She was talking on the phone, but she waved me inside, motioned for me to sit in the chair opposite her, and mouthed but did not say the word "resume."

I clicked open my briefcase and retrieved a copy of it for her.

"No, no," the woman said into the phone, while reaching out a hand for my resume. "That's not how it works, and you know it, Charles. Speak to my lawyer. Don't call here again. And may I offer you a piece of advice? Just sign the damned paperwork so each of us can move on with our lives. It's been months since I've filed. I'm tired of this. I want you out of my life. So do the children. God!"

Without another word, she hung up the phone, looked down at my resume, and then looked back at me, anger clearly stamped on her face. "Ms. Kent," she said. "Hellohoware?"

"I'm fine, Ms. Blackwell. Thank you for seeing me."

"There's no need to thank me. It's what I do. All day long. Sometimes on weekends." She scanned the resume. "You're from Maine?"

"I am."

"And you graduated in May?"

"With my master's degree, yes."

"In business?"

"That's right."

She looked at me. "Why would you be interested in a secretarial job when you have an MBA?"

I tried to keep myself composed. "I've been here since May, and it's been difficult to find a job."

"You are aware that the economy is in the toilet, aren't you?"

"I am. I just thought that there would be more opportunities here than in Maine."

"Which brings you to me today."

"That's right."

"Here's how I view this. You want to answer phones until you can find a better job. Why would I waste my time on that? That will just mean replacing your position sooner rather than later."

I could feel myself flush. "Actually, I was hoping this would be a way to get my foot in the door. I was hoping that if I worked hard enough at Wenn, that someone might see something in me that would allow for other opportunities to open."

"Is that so? And how long would you give us for that to happen? A few weeks? A couple of months? Until you found work elsewhere?"

"If the pay was decent, I'd wait until something good opened up."

"Well, that's kind of you."

"Ms. Blackwell, I'm a good worker. I just need a chance. If I don't find a job soon, I'll need to move back to Maine and give up my dreams here."

"And that concerns me how?" She tossed the resume back on her desk. "Look, Ms. Kent. I'm not looking for a short-term hire. I'm looking for someone to fill this position for the long-term so I don't have to fill it again for another year or so. Does that make sense? You're not in Maine anymore. You're in New York. It's a big city filled with lots of people just like you who are trying to find work. Spare me the theatrics about "just needing a chance." That's already being sold in every show on Broadway. I suggest you get a ticket to a matinee and soak it up."

What was her problem? "Did I do something to offend you?"

"You've wasted my time."

"Actually, I think I walked into an argument."

"You think you walked into a what?"

"An argument. You were arguing when I walked in. Now, you're taking it out on me. That's unprofessional. I'm not Charles, so please stop acting as if I am."

The woman sat back in her chair and looked amused. "Well, look at you, Maine. Maybe you do have what it takes to make it in the big city. That's quite a mouth you have on you." She leaned forward and a lock of her black hair fell into her face. "But we're not going to listen to it here. Have a nice day."

Furious, I stood. Really? A three-minute interview? What had I done to deserve this? How many times was I going to be dismissed in this city? I felt another flash of anger, and directed it at this Blackwell bitch just as she had directed her anger at me. "Have a swell divorce. From where I sit, it looks like Charles got away from a dragon."

"Sweetheart, you have no idea. And thanks for your resume. I'll be sure to call all the headhunters I know around town and warn them about you."

"So, you'd like another lawsuit?"

"Oh, please. From what you told me, you couldn't afford it. Goodbye, Ms. Kent. Goodbye and good luck. Now, go on. Close your mouth. Ms. Blackwell is finished with you. Toodles."

CHAPTER FOUR

Shaken by the exchange, I left the woman's office and walked blindly down the hallway to the bank of elevators. Dozens of men and women either were walking toward me, or moving past me, and all of them had jobs. *What is wrong with me? Why can't I land one? I'm almost out of money. If I don't find something soon, I don't know what I'll do.*

I felt tears sting my eyes, but I was damned if I was going to cry, so I blinked them away.

You're better than this. This isn't it for you. That was all her. Listen to Lisa. Think about a waitressing gig. That could give you the time you need to get the job you want. You've got experience waitressing. You need the money. Focus on that.

I went to one of the elevators and pressed the down button. Despite the air conditioning, I felt hotter than I had in my apartment. I stood waiting for the elevator to come, and couldn't help but hear my father's voice in my head.

You're gonna fail, you know? You're gonna fail and you're gonna come runnin' back to us. Well, here's the deal, girl. We might not have you back if you fail. Your mother and I might just be fine without you. Think about that if you leave.

It was, in fact, that conversation which convinced me to leave. Lisa and I had graduated the week before. I called to tell her what my father had said, and by the end of that week, we had secured our shitty little apartment through a Realtor in New York, we had packed Lisa's ten-year-old Golf, which we long ago nicknamed Gretta, and we had left Maine and our former lives behind,

"Gretta will get us out of here," Lisa said when we hit I-95 South. "She might be old, but she never lets me down. We'll do this together. My book is finished, the cover is killer, but the text needs a solid proof from you before I load it onto Amazon. Who knows what will happen to it? Maybe it'll hit. But even if it doesn't, we have each other, just as we always have. We'll figure this out together. Don't let your drunk ass of a father derail you from your dreams. And, please, don't let him get further into your head and fuck you up more than he already has."

Easier said than done. My father's words haunted me every bit as much now as they always did. Maybe he saw the real Jennifer Kent. Maybe he saw me for who I really was—a failure. Someone who after four months couldn't land a damn job in one of the world's largest cities to save her life.

The elevator doors whisked open. No one was inside, which was a blessing. I entered the car, pressed the button for the lobby, and leaned back against the elevator wall.

I'm not going to cry.

But I did. I was angry, I was overwhelmed, and I felt that I had no choice but to find a job as a server at a fine-dining restaurant. This, of course, would mean another round of interviews because I needed to find a great restaurant that paid well. I felt deflated at the prospect of having to start all over again. My eyes again started to well up in frustration.

To my horror, just when my emotions got the best of me, the elevator slowed as it approached the forty-seventh floor. I quickly wiped the tears from my eyes, worrying that in the process I had smeared my mascara, and I lowered my head as the doors opened so no one could see the truth on my face about how deeply sad, angry, and desperate I was.

Only I wasn't so quick. For an instant, the man who stepped inside the car locked eyes with me. He looked at me with concern, saw that the button for the lobby was already lit, and stood next to me.

The doors slid shut. An uncomfortable silence stretched between us.

He was gorgeous. Of course, he was. Why wouldn't he be gorgeous? Why should the universe stop kicking my ass now?

It only took a glance to see how handsome he was. Probably six-foot-two, gleaming dark hair raked away from a chiseled face peppered with stubble, full lips, and eyes that were the color of the sea. They were his best feature—blue-green and framed by thick lashes. I'd seen plenty of attractive men during my time in Manhattan, the lot of which I ignored because I needed to find a job before I even thought about the prospect of dating. But this man was beyond my type. Given my overwhelming streak of good luck, naturally I was a complete mess when he first saw me.

Get me out of here. Please, just let the elevator move faster and get me to the street. I'll walk home in the heat. I don't care. Just get me out of here now.

"I'm sorry," he said. "But are you all right?"

Fuck my life. "I'm afraid my allergies have gotten the best of me today. My eyes are burning."

"Is that it?"

He knows better. He knows I'm lying. So, what the hell? He's a stranger. According to Ms. Blackwell, I'll never see her or him again. Why not burn her while I have the chance? Maybe it'll get back to her.

"Actually, that's not true."

"What is true?"

"I came here for a secretarial job. I have my master's degree in business, I've been in New York since May, and nothing has worked out. I can't find a job. Apparently—according to Ms. Blackwell on the fifty-first floor, who obviously is so pissed that she's going through a nasty divorce that she took it out on me—I can't even take phone calls or manage a filing system. Give me a break. I was hoping to get my foot in the door here and work my way up, but today turned out to be just another day of disappointment." I looked at him, saw what looked like irritation on his face, and managed a smile. "Sorry to vent."

"I'm the one who asked the question. You met with Ms. Blackwell?"

"Yes, but don't go near her. She's Hell on Earth. She threatened contact the headhunters she knows in the city and warn them about me."

His brow furrowed. I could see the anger in his eyes. "Why would she do that?"

"Because she couldn't imagine why I'd be interested in a low-level job that I'm over-qualified for. She said I'd wasted her time. We exchanged words. It wasn't pretty, but she wasn't professional. She made it personal. So, now I'll be damaged goods to any headhunter I might reach out to."

"What she did is libelous."

"It is. Not that I can do anything about it. I'm broke." I took a breath and changed the subject. This guy wasn't only smoking hot, but he seemed kind and sincere, not unlike the cab driver who brought me here. I loved this city. But right now? Because of Blackwell? It could go to Hell.

I reached behind my head and released the clip that had held my hair up and away from my face. I shook it out and let it fall over my shoulders in soft brown waves. It felt freeing.

"How do you like it here?" I asked him. "Assuming you're an employee. Am I missing out on something great? Despite the black witch of death back there, I feel as if I am."

He was looking at my hair, but then he appeared to check himself and he met my eyes. "Working here wasn't exactly part of my own plan, but here I am. It's OK. It keeps me busy, which is important."

"What do you do?"

"Just business stuff. I won't bore you with it."

"I'd loved to be bored with 'just business stuff'."

I admired his expensive suit and the gleaming watch at his wrist, and decided he likely was a senior director or something whose work was intense. I looked fleetingly at his face, saw him looking intently at mine, and I couldn't deny my attraction to him. How old was he? Thirty? Could he be single? Looking like that, there was no way that he was single. Unless he preferred it that way. Not that it mattered. He was in a completely different league than me—the cost of his watch alone probably could keep me in my apartment for the next year—so when the elevator started to slow, I was relieved. I really just wanted to get home.

"What's your name?" he asked.

As hot as he was, I never gave out my full name to just anyone. "It's Jennifer," I said. I didn't want to know his, so I didn't ask.

But he offered anyway.

"I'm Alex."

He extended his hand, which I shook as the elevator stopped and the doors opened.

"It was nice meeting you," I said, aware of the spark I felt when we touched. The palm of his hand was smooth and unusually warm. "Again, sorry for venting."

"It sounds as if you had every reason to."

Was this guy for real? A part of me didn't want to leave, but I did. I had to get home and start hitting the streets for a waitressing gig. I didn't have time for men, not even this one.

"Have a nice day," I said.

We stepped out of the elevator together. I quickened my step to move ahead of him, but I could sense him behind me. I could hear his footfalls. I could feel his eyes on me. With my briefcase in my right hand, I ran my left hand down the length of my suit to make sure it wasn't wrinkled when I walked outside. I pulled down my jacket, combed my fingers through my hair, and shook it out. I pushed open the door, and waited for him to grab it behind me. He didn't. When I turned to see where he was, I saw him standing at the door with his hands in his pockets. He was smiling at me.

I smiled back, and then, to my horror, I collided with someone on the sidewalk.

My briefcase was knocked out of my hand, and it fell to the ground with such force that it sprang open. In the sudden suction of air, the extra resumes I kept within the case were set free and started to swirl down Fifth. The older man I walked into told me to watch where I was going, and he walked away, annoyed.

"Jesus," I said to myself. I quickly started to catch whatever resumes I could. It cost a lot of money to have them printed on good paper. Money I didn't have to print them off again. I'd need them later when I started to interview at restaurants. "I can't believe this," I said.

The door swung open behind me. "We'll never get all of them," I heard him say. "But we can get some of them back. Here. Let me help."

To my surprise, he jogged down Fifth, where he weaved through the crowds on the wide sidewalk and picked up whatever resumes were still within reach. I did the same. As we finished, I watched him stroll up the avenue toward me, several resumes clutched in his hand. On his face was a sheen of sweat. It was hot as hell outside, but he was more than enough to make that heat feel like an icicle. He looked like a God to me. I couldn't remember being this physically drawn to a man. In fact, I'd never felt this way before. I generally dismissed men.

"Are you OK?" he asked.

"I'm fine," I said. "Embarrassed, but fine. Thanks so much." I took the resumes from him. "You didn't need to do that."

"Apparently, the guy you bumped into wasn't going to help you. It was an honest mistake. Sometimes I don't understand why people need to be so rude."

"This day needs to end," I said. "Thanks again. I appreciate it, Alex." Feeling like an idiot, I closed my briefcase, said a quick, awkward goodbye, and walked away from him, even though I sensed that he was about to say something to me when I turned to leave.

CHAPTER FIVE

When I arrived back at my apartment, I was a sweaty mess. I had soaked through my shirt and parts of my jacket, my hair was damp and stuck to my forehead, the area between my thighs felt raw, and my feet. Good God, my feet. In three-inch heels, I'd just walked several miles in ninety-degree heat. I had a feeling that when my shoes came off—if I could even get the damned things off due to the obvious swelling—I would face some serious blisters.

I climbed the four flights of stairs to my apartment, which just about killed me. I put my key into the lock, opened the door and found Lisa banging away on her Mac.

It was clear that she was on a roll. So as quietly as possible, I put my briefcase down on the kitchen counter, took off my shoes, saw spots of blood on the inside and several blisters near my toes, and frowned at the sight. This was ridiculous. I had just ruined perfectly good shoes and maybe even my only really good suit. This was no way to live. I needed to do something about this fast.

I had planned on taking a shower before checking out a few restaurants online to see which were among the best, but that obviously wasn't happening with my feet in this condition. I needed to take care of them so they wouldn't become infected. Without disturbing Lisa, I could take a shower, tend to my feet, and then Google some of the better restaurants in the city. If they had a "careers" link, I'd see if they were hiring.

"How's it going, Jennifer?"

Lisa was still typing like a fiend, but then she had that ability to focus on work and still hold a conversation if the words were rushing out of her, as they were now.

"You don't even want to know. Look at me."

"Can't. Come over here. Stand in front of me."

Wincing, I walked over and stood in front of Lisa. She glanced up once, turned back to her laptop, and then stopped all together when she shot me a second look.

"Holy hell! You look like shit. And you never look like shit. What happened?"

I sat in the chair opposite her and told her everything.

"How did you manage for all of that to happen within a few hours?"

"I'm gifted that way."

"I'm sorry about Blackwell. What a bitch."

"There's a special sort of Hell for a person like that. Soon, the fires will nip at her ass."

"Singe it."

"Burn it."

"Make toast of it."

"Blister it worse than my feet." I stuck out my legs. "Check out these beauties."

"Oh, Jennifer, I'm so sorry. You don't deserve this. You need to take care of those now."

"I'm taking a cold shower in a few minutes."

"There's hydrogen peroxide in the cabinet. Use it. You don't want to find yourself in a hospital with an infection."

I saluted her. "Not that I have health insurance or could afford it. But noted, boss."

"So, who is this guy?"

"Lisa, you should have seen him."

"You never talk about men. Ever. I totally get the physical attraction thing—it can knock you senseless, make you stupid and essentially destroy your life, as I know perfectly well from my last two relationships— so I can only assume that he was gorgeous."

"He was. Tall, dark, and handsome to the tenth degree. Blue-green eyes. Body to die for. This really sexy stubble on his face. And he was kind. Maybe that's what really did me in. He seemed like a sweet guy. Generally, the two don't go together. Is there a disconnect there, or is it just me?"

"Maybe he was being kind because he got a look at your ass."

"Leave my butt out of this."

"I just wish I was packing what you're packing. I'm as flat as my mother is, and you know what that looks like." She looked at me. "You know, I wasn't joking. You never talk about men. I know the reasons why, but this is unusual."

"What can I say? I've never felt like that before. He was amazing. Totally my type. And obviously wealthy, which means we're on opposite ends of the financial spectrum, and thus not compatible. But, God, what a stud. Well dressed. This beautiful, masculine watch on his wrist. Great shoes. Groomed to perfection. And there I was, turning back to look at him with my stupid smiling face, only to collide with some fat old fart who nearly flattened me right then and there on the sidewalk. I'm such a class act, someone should write a paper about me. You just don't see class like this every day."

"So, how did you end it?"

"I walked home."

"You didn't exchange numbers?"

"Are you serious? Lisa, I need to focus and get myself out of this mess. He was a hunk with nice manners, but that's where it ends."

"At some point, you're going to have to trust someone enough to let it begin."

I looked at her but said nothing, even though I knew she was right. At some point, I needed to let it all go.

"Go take a shower," she said. "I'm worried about infection setting in, especially in this heat. You know I write about zombies. If your feet get infected, it might lead to the wrong kind of infection. And then what are we going to do?" She winked at me. "Seriously, your feet are swollen and they don't look good. Please go and take care of them, or I will."

"Will do. And thanks for the cab fare. I have a story to tell you about that later."

"I told you not to worry about it."

"But I do. When I get out of the shower, I'm going to start researching restaurants online to find out which are the best and whether they are hiring."

"You've got the experience. Lord knows you've got the looks. I think after your feet are better, your best marketing campaign is going to be your appearance in person. You present well. In this profession, your looks will matter to them. That, and your ability to serve their clients. This line of work will be profitable for you, and it's a good option until you find what you're looking for."

To my surprise, when Lisa said that, it wasn't a job that flashed before her eyes, but Alex's face.

CHAPTER SIX

In the morning, after an overnight treatment of antibiotic ointments that Lisa bought for me at the pharmacy down the street, my feet looked better. Much better, which was a relief. The blisters were still in full bloody bloom and they looked like a horror show, but the swelling was way down, and that meant that any infection was in check.

So, no hospitals for me. I couldn't afford to visit one anyway, and I also couldn't afford to lose time. I needed to get up, make a pot of coffee for each of us, and give Lisa a hug for helping to apply the ointment and wrap my foot with gauze. Then, I needed to start searching the Web for the best restaurants in the city. I certainly wasn't going to shuck food at something like Tubby's Diner. I needed a top restaurant where I could pull in enough cash to replenish my anemic bank account, which now had the distinct whiff of the pathetic.

And I was willing to work my ass off for that.

If I was going to survive in this city—and not go home, where my parents would either ridicule or reject me—I needed money. Quick money, as in tip money. If I could get into the best place possible, I knew things would turn around for me because it would give me a chance to find the job I wanted during the day. It wouldn't be easy, but it sure as hell would keep me here, which is where I wanted to stay.

And thank you again, Lisa, for the idea.

I wanted to treat her. I slid out of bed and stepped quietly into the kitchen. My feet hurt like hell, but not as bad as they had yesterday. I found her sleeping on the pullout, and I felt guilty about it. Here she was making the most money between us, and she didn't have the bedroom. Looking at her sleeping, her blonde hair swept like a net across her pretty face, I decided that I'd give her the bedroom. She deserved it. When we first arrived in Manhattan, she just assumed that I was the one who'd get the well-paying job, and that she'd hope for the best with her book.

"You take the bedroom," she had said. "I don't know how this book will do. You'll be making more money than me in no time. It's only fair."

Only, that wasn't the case now. As far as I was concerned, the bedroom was hers, and I'd sleep on the pullout. And frankly, who cared? What mattered was our friendship. One day, we'd be beyond this ridiculousness, and would laugh about it over martinis at the Ritz.

You keep dreaming, girl.

I'm going to.

Then dream big.

I plan to. I didn't save up for years to come here for nothing. I came here to make it.

When the coffee started to brew, the aroma was enough to wake Lisa.

"That smells amazing," she said.

"And it's only Folgers. Imagine if it was Starbucks."

A dreamy look came over her face. "Starbucks," she said. "If I were a zombie—which I might be after the Chapter I wrote last night—that's the first place I'd go. I'd have a Java Chip Frappuccino, a cookie, and obviously a side of brains, because, you know,

I'd be a zombie. So, let's imagine that it's Starbucks."

"You're the creative one," I said. "It'll be a snap for you. For me, not so much. But, hey, at least we have coffee!"

She started to get up.

"No," I said. "Stay there. I'll bring you a cup. You've been a lifesaver these past couple of weeks. Or months. Mostly months. Enjoy your last few moments on the pullout, because tonight the bedroom is yours."

She sat up in bed and looked at me. "What are you talking about?"

"The bedroom is yours. It's only right. I'll move my stuff into your closet, and you can move everything of yours into the bedroom closet. Decorate the room, enjoy a real bed for once, and sleep like the princess you are."

"Jennifer, you don't have to do that. I don't mind sleeping here. Actually, because of the bar that cuts across the mattress, it actually makes me get up and start writing earlier than I would have otherwise. That bar is pure motivation."

I nodded toward the bedroom. "I believe there's an alarm clock in there."

"With a snooze button."

I rolled my eyes, poured us two cups of coffee, and added some sugar and then some creamer. After a brisk stir, I brought her a cup, and kissed her on the forehead. "Seriously. I've been a handful lately. More than usual, which means you've had a mountain on your hands. I appreciate all you've done for me—more than you know—and I especially appreciate your patience. I've been a mess."

She screwed up her face at me. "You don't have to thank me. I think you listened to me for weeks when Kevin dumped me. Remember what that was like? Let me remind you, because it was epic. 'Why would he ever want to leave a hot piece of ass like this? What a fool. What an idiot. Who is he kidding? I mean, right? Right? This is bullshit. Ughhhh. Why do I still love him? Why do I wish he'd call me right now? I'm going to kill him. Help me slash the tires on that fucking car of his. I'll get a knife.' And on and on. I was a drunk psycho bitch without a filter that night. This friendship isn't exactly one-sided, and you know it never has been."

I sat down on the chair at the end of her bed. "When you're ready to switch rooms, let me know, OK? But it has to be today. It's my turn on the sofa."

She was about to speak, but I raised a hand. "Please don't. You deserve it. I insist. That's the end of it. Now, let me tell you about my day." I told her about my plans to narrow down the best restaurants in the city and—when my feet were able to handle a pair of shoes—to start visiting them ASAP for a job.

"I think you're making the right move."

"It was your idea. And it is the right move. Hell, I'll probably make more waitressing than I would have if I wound up working for the evil Ms. Blackwell. And if I do get a job, I'm buying the air conditioner. Can you believe this heat? Even this early in the morning? I should open some windows. Get some air moving."

"Maybe for an hour."

"Cool it off before it becomes too much."

"It's supposed to be over ninety again today."

I smiled at her. "Then I suggest we both double up on the deodorant. Otherwise, we're both screwed."

My cell phone rang as I was opening the living room window.

"Who's calling me at this hour?"

"Maybe it's for a job. Maybe you're getting a call back."

I got up and crossed into the kitchen where my phone was on the counter. "Don't make me nervous."

"Who is it?"

I just stared at the screen. "Wenn Enterprises," I said. "Holy shit, you're right. It's Blackwell."

CHAPTER SEVEN

"Hello?"

"Jennifer Kent?"

I looked over at Lisa and nodded. It was Blackwell, all right. The clipped tone of her voice was immediately recognizable. "This is she."

"This is Ms. Blackwell."

"Who?"

"Ms. Blackwell."

"I'm sorry, I'm drawing a blank."

"Really? I can't imagine." She cleared her throat, likely out of anger and frustration. "A position has recently opened. I was asked to call to see if you were interested in coming in for an interview."

"I'm sorry. Where is this interview?"

"Wenn Enterprises."

"Oh, you're that Ms. Blackwell."

"That's right."

"How could I forget? The one who threatened me? The one who used her divorce against me? I'm afraid I'm busy, Ms. Blackwell."

"I'd think twice about that, Ms. Kent."

"And why is that?"

"Because this job is special. It's a high-paying job. It's the sort of job that will help you get noticed at Wenn Enterprises, which I believe you said you wanted when we first met."

"You mean, when we first exchanged words?"

"Ms. Kent, I apologize for the way I treated you." It was as if she was reading a script. Her voice was cold and tight. Nothing in her tone suggested that she was sorry at all, but damned if she wasn't going through the motions. *Why?* "It was an unfortunate exchange that we had the other day. That's all. I've been under some pressure lately."

"So, I noted. And that affects me how?"

"It shouldn't have affected you at all, thus my apology."

Whatever. "Why are you calling me about this job again?"

"I was asked to."

"By whom?"

"By Mr. Wenn himself. He saw your resume. He'd like you to come in for an interview."

"How did Mr. Wenn, of all people, see my resume?"

"I can't disclose that."

"Is this for the secretarial position?"

"No. He's in need of an executive assistant."

"Doesn't he already have one?"

"He did, but he promoted her this morning."

"To what?"

"Senior director of something or other."

"That's specific."

"Ms. Kent, I didn't order the promotion. Mr. Wenn did. I was recently told about it, and then I was instructed to call you. That's all I know."

"But why didn't you warn him against me? This doesn't make sense. You cast me out of your office. You said I wasn't worth your time. You must have told Mr. Wenn that. You said—I believe—'toodles' to me."

"And I've apologized. I'm hoping we can get beyond that. I'm calling to ask you if you'd like to interview for the job."

"Before I come in, Ms. Blackwell, I need to know what the position entails."

"You'll serve Mr. Wenn. This isn't just about keeping his calendar. Though you'll do that, in a way. Probably the best way to describe this position is that you'll be his confidante. You'll be that one indispensable person he can't live without. In this particular case, that's what Mr. Wenn needs. You'll literally be his right arm. As you'd imagine, he's a busy man. He needs someone bright to step in and help him keep sense of things. He needs someone he can bounce ideas off of. After seeing your resume, he was intrigued because he needs someone who is as well educated as you are. You'll work long hours together. Late hours. You need to be prepared for that."

"How many hours?"

"At least twelve. Likely up to fifteen per day. And you'll work most weekends. Mr. Wenn works very hard."

He's a billionaire. Why wouldn't he? "That seems excessive."

"In New York, it isn't, Ms. Kent. Though I imagine that it is in Maine."

I ignored the slight. Mainers often worked three jobs to pay the bills, and some still were at the poverty level. This woman didn't know what she was talking about. "What is the pay?"

"Two hundred fifty thousand per year."

My mouth dropped open. Was she joking? Of course, she was. This was a joke. A cruel one. When I didn't say anything, she said, "I assume you're surprised by the pay?"

I collected myself. "Actually, no. It's Wenn Enterprises, after all. I'd expect the pay to be at that level for an executive position."

"Right. Well, Ms. Kent, I need to ask if you're willing to come in for an interview. You'll be meeting directly with Mr. Wenn. The interview will last an hour. Are you interested?"

I decided to go for it. "Is the pay negotiable?"

"Everything is negotiable, especially if he feels that you're the right person for the job. But I wouldn't push it. You have no real-world experience."

"Apparently, I have enough experience to command two hundred fifty thousand dollars a year."

Lisa's mouth fell open and I looked away before she could throw me off my game.

"Perhaps. May I schedule an appointment?"

With my feet in such terrible condition, I could barely walk. I needed to put this off for a few days so they could have time to heal. Otherwise, I'd come off like an idiot. "How does Thursday sound?"

"We were hoping that you'd come in this afternoon."

"I have a funeral to attend this afternoon. The burial is tomorrow. It will need to be Thursday."

"I'll let Mr. Wenn know about the funeral and the burial, and I'll call you back."

Before I could say another word, the line went dead.

I turned to Lisa and was about to scream when the line rang again. "You've got to be kidding me?" I said.

"Answer it!"

"That quick?"

"Just answer it!"

I took a breath. "This is Jennifer."

"Thursday at noon, Ms. Kent. Mr. Wenn would like to send flowers to the deceased. Can you please give me the name of the funeral home?"

Was he standing right next to her? Only moments had lapsed between calls. "That's unnecessary."

"But he insists."

Shit. "Please tell him that I appreciate the gesture, but this isn't a relative of mine. I'm going to the funeral to support a friend. I'll see Mr. Wenn at noon on Thursday. I assume I come to you first?"

"You do."

"Thank you, Ms. Blackwell."

The woman paused, and I could sense the temperature in the room dropping twenty degrees.

"Good luck, Ms. Kent."

CHAPTER EIGHT

"Jennifer, just hear me out, OK? Just listen to me. No talking. I need you to be focused. Are you focused? Oh, shit, you're not focused. Why would you be? Put down the phone. Step away from it. And listen to me. Can you do that? Apparently, not. Why are you looking so pale? Jesus, don't faint."

I was in a haze. From potential waitress to potential cash cow in a matter of minutes. I blinked into a room in which the edges were oddly blurred. I felt light headed, as if I'd had a drink. The world seemed to be turning on its axis. I could hear the sound of something rushing in my ears. "Two hundred and fifty thousand dollars. A year. Oh my God."

Lisa gripped my arm in an effort to steady me. "You don't have the job yet."

"I need to get this job."

She pressed me back against the counter and held me there for support. "Then listen to me. You have a credit card. You haven't used it since we got here. You saved it for an emergency. Well, this is an emergency. Do you hear me? This is a full-on, five-alarm-fire emergency. You need to have your hair cut and colored. You need to buy a new suit and shoes—and nothing cheap. If it doesn't work out, you can pay off the clothes and the haircut with the waitressing gig you'll land. Are you listening to me? What's wrong with your eyes? Why are you smiling at me like that? Jennifer? Jennifer!"

"I can't believe it."

"Snap out of it."

"I don't even know what that kind of money looks like. My parents are poor. I've always been poor. What the hell does it feel like to make that much money?"

"You won't know if you don't listen to me."

"Why would they pay me so much right off the bat?"

"Who cares? Maybe that's what they pay in New York. What's the job, anyway?"

"Executive Assistant to Mr. Wenn."

"There's your reason."

"She said I'd be working twelve to fifteen hours a day. Including most weekends. Apparently, I'm about to become his right-armed confidante."

"What does that mean? Never mind. Come over here and sit down. Drink your coffee. If it's cold, I'll pour you another cup. But I need you to sit down. You can't walk in there with a smashed nose if you suddenly decide to collapse on me."

I felt Lisa guide me across the room and I was gently lowered into a chair.

"Take a breath."

I breathed in deeply. "Taken."

"Now, come on. Drink your coffee and get it together. Enough is enough."

I did as I was told, and slowly fell back into myself. "Sorry," I said. "That was unfortunate."

"You may have just won the lottery. I get it. It's a lot to absorb, but you're not even there yet. What you have is an opportunity. That's it. Today, you rest. Tomorrow, we get your hair done. Then we buy a new suit and shoes. I'm talking Prada and Louboutins. OK?"

I nodded at her. "I can't believe this."

"Well, believe it. You've waited months for this opportunity."

"I sure as hell wasn't expecting *this* opportunity."

"All the sweeter. I'm going to get a clean towel and wash your feet. Then, I'll apply more ointment and wrap them again with gauze. We'll do it again before you go to bed. Ibuprofen will take care of the rest of the swelling. You'll take two pills every four hours. We need to get you back on your feet as quickly as possible."

I looked her in the eyes. "Can you believe this?" I asked.

"Yes," she said. "But I've always believed in you. You're the one who doesn't. You and your parents. But I'm proud of you. Beyond proud of you. This could be it. Now, we need to make sure this is it. Got me?"

"Got you," I said.

"Prada fixes everything," she said. "Or at least, that's what I hear. Usually, a martini does it for me. But in this case, I'll listen to the Bible, which naturally is this month's edition of *Vogue*. I devoured it last week. Prada's new line is on trend. Queen Wintour never gets it wrong."

CHAPTER NINE

It was a rare girls' day out, and despite the sorry condition of my feet, which were still sore even in the most comfortable and forgiving flats that I owned, Lisa and I made a day of it.

My hair was styled and colored by Salon V on East Seventh Street. Nothing dramatic, just enough to complement the oval shape of my face, with a chestnut color that enhanced the look. I treated each of us to a facial and a mani-pedi.

"We're in the wrong business," Lisa said when the bill was tallied and I paid the cashier with my credit card. "Good grief."

"It'll be worth it," I said.

"You look amazing."

"She's right," the cashier said. "You do. I wish I looked like you."

I smiled at her. "That's very kind of you."

"Trust me. It's the truth."

I flushed at the compliment. "I need to look my best." I looked at Lisa, who was wearing skinny jeans, red double-strap patent-leather sandals, and a white tank with nothing beneath it save for her full breasts and a clear view of her nipples.

As racy as she looked, it was a look she could pull off. Her blonde hair was pulled away from her face in a simple ponytail that fell to the small of her back. With the exception of mascara, she wore almost no makeup because she didn't need much. To me, she was the pretty one. She studied style and loved fashion, and it came easily to her, which made me smile because otherwise her life revolved around successfully writing about zombies.

"Do you think I did the right thing by keeping most of the length?"

"You can do more with your hair that way. Any number of things. And your split ends are history. Thank God for that. One day, you and your cheap shampoo will part."

"I haven't done this since we left Maine. I was way overdue for all of it. And if the job at Wenn doesn't work out, it will just help me when I look for a waitressing gig."

"A server gig?"

"Right."

"And it will. But you're going to land this job, so we won't think of the other right now. It's all about confidence. Looking like you do now, you should be filled with it."

But I wasn't. I wondered if that day would ever come.

On Lisa's dime, we took a cab to Prada on Fifth Avenue. After trying on six different outfits, I bought a pale blue suit with a white silk top that fit perfectly and worked well with my hair color and skin tone. The suit was nearly three thousand dollars, though I scored big when we found some discounted leather point-toe Prada pumps that cost a third of what the Louboutins would have cost me. I had to hold my breath when I paid for them. What was I doing? Today had cost me a fortune I didn't have.

I'm doing the right thing. I'm investing in my future.

At least I hoped that was the case.

After finishing our cheap salads and Diet Cokes at a corner table at McDonald's—we had to make a concession somewhere on this ridiculously expensive day—Lisa grilled me with leading questions in an effort to prepare me for tomorrow's interview. When she finished, she seemed pleased by the answers.

"Well, there's one thing that can be said for the past four months," she said.

"What's that?"

"Because you've had so many interviews, you're more than prepared for whatever comes tomorrow. It's as if you have your master's degree in interviewing. Whatever he lobs at you, you'll be prepared for it."

"Do you think so?"

"I know so."

Neither of us could have known then how wrong she was.

CHAPTER TEN

At ten minutes before noon, I arrived at Wenn Enterprises by cab. The taxi was yet another treat from Lisa. I owed her big time. Not just for the financial support, but also for the emotional support. To make certain that my feet returned home without additional swelling and blisters, she gave me enough cab fare for a ride back to the apartment as well. There was no better friend. I was blessed to have her in my life and in my corner.

If I get this job, she is so going to be spoiled with a shopping extravaganza that will annihilate anything in her zombie-apocalypse world.

I left the cab, and approached the building, clicking toward it with my new shoes, which were beyond beyond. I'd never splurged on shoes like these because, frankly, I couldn't afford them. They were elegant, chic, and surprisingly comfortable. I was relieved that my feet were nearly back to normal. But as I crossed the sidewalk, I couldn't forget what happened the last time I was here: My moment with Ms. Blackwell. My briefcase smashing onto the sidewalk. Resumes flying everywhere. And that God of a man rushing out of the building to help me retrieve them. All in all, coming here that day had turned out to be one of the worst days I've had since I'd arrived in Manhattan. And now here I was again, invited back to interview for a position that could change my life for the foreseeable future. Surreal didn't even begin to describe how I felt.

I crossed the lobby to the reception desk, and tossed my hair neatly behind me. I had decided to wear it down. The way it was skillfully cut, it just looked better that way, especially with my newly chestnut hair contrasting against my pale blue suit.

"I'm Jennifer Kent," I said to one of the men behind the desk.

"Sorry?"

There were too many people in the lobby. I needed to speak up. "I'm Jennifer Kent. I have an interview with Mr. Wenn today."

"Which means you need to see Ms. Blackwell."

Terrific. But I knew that was coming.

"Let me call and let her know that you're here."

"Thank you."

He acted as if he didn't even hear me. Instead, he spoke into the phone. "A Ms. Kent is here to see you. Waiting room? Oh. OK. I'll have her come straight to you."

He hung up the phone, and said, "Fifty-First floor. Hang a left. Down a long hallway. You'll find—"

"I've been there," I said, dreading the moment when Ms. Blackwell would belittle me again. "I can find Ms. Blackwell." *I can sniff her out like a dog on a bone.* "Thank you."

This time, he actually smiled at me. "My pleasure, Ms. Kent."

* * *

When I arrived at Blackwell's office, she looked up at me, took in my hair and suit, and then she held up a hand. She was on the phone again, just like the last time.

"Max, here's what you need to know, which is what you already know, but which you can't seem to

get through that thick head of yours, so I'll do you
the favor of repeating it again. Charles isn't getting
my money. *I'm* getting *his* money. Got that? God!
He's the one who screwed around on the living room
floor with that slut from Saks. That was documented
by our nanny cam and I have the footage of it. What
more evidence do you need to nail this down? What's
more damaging than what I've already given to you?
Nothing! I suggest you man up and get the job done,
or I'm firing you and going with another lawyer.
Don't give me attitude, Max. Don't sigh. Don't
grumble. We both know what's in this for you. We
both know that you'll make a killing off this. So, just
shut up, grow a pair, and get me out of this marriage
by the end of the week. You've got until Friday. If
you screw it up, I'm going elsewhere. Lots of lawyers
would like me to go elsewhere. Oh, good day to you,
too, you son of a bitch. Get it done!"

She hung up the phone and looked up at me not
with the irritation I was expecting, but with an
exhausted look on her face. "Don't ever get married."

I didn't reply.

"But you don't want to hear that," she said,
looking up at me. "You're here to see Mr. Wenn."

"I am."

She pushed back her chair and stood. "You look nice today. I like the suit."

"Thanks."

"Looks expensive."

"It was."

"And here I thought you were poor."

"I am. But credit cards can alleviate that."

"A momentary illusion. Can I give you a suggestion?"

"Of course."

"Do you mind if I touch you?"

"You need to touch me for a suggestion?"

"Just your hair. Trust me on this."

Trust the Kraken? "OK...."

She plucked a shiny black stick from the silver-plated pen-and-pencil holder in front of her, came up behind me and lifted my hair off my back. With a twist and a curl, she raised it up, flipped it over, turned it again, and speared my hair with the stick, creating what felt to me like a tight chignon.

"There's a mirror there," she said, pointing to the wall at my left. "Have a look."

I was right—it was a chignon. And it looked good. As much as I liked my hair loose around my shoulders, this look was more polished and sophisticated.

"I like it," I said. "Thank you."

"Another tip?" she said.

I looked at her.

"In the middle of the interview, when you understand the situation and you know the moment is right, pull out the stick and let your hair fall behind you. Do it naturally. Do it absentmindedly. Do it while you're talking to him, and make it seem as if it's the last thing on your mind. Keep your eyes on his while you do it."

"What do you mean by 'understand the situation'?"

"You'll see."

"What's the point of letting down my hair?"

"You're about to get the point, Ms. Kent. I'm just trying to help."

"So, I have to ask the obvious. After our last exchange, why would you want to help me?"

"Because we all make mistakes. Because I was having a rough day when we first met. I took it out on you, and I apologize for it. I've been where you are now. I understand what's coming."

"What's coming is just a job interview," I said.

She smiled at me, and behind that smile was a mystery that was reflected—but not revealed—in her eyes. "That's right. So, how about if we go and see Mr. Wenn now? I know he's eager to meet you."

CHAPTER ELEVEN

We left her office and walked down the long hallway to the bank of elevators. Ms. Blackwell pressed the down button. The elevator door opened after a moment, I stepped in after her, and she pressed the button for the forty-seventh floor.

Nothing was said between us. I touched the back of my hair and felt almost faint with anticipation.

There was so much riding on this interview. I could feel my heart ram against my chest. Worse, my father was in my head: *Good luck, girl. You're going to need it.*

What I needed to do was focus. What I needed to do was to believe in myself and not mess this up. Lisa was right. At this point, I was a master at interviewing, even if I'd yet to land a job. The questions were almost always the same: "What's your greatest weakness?" "Why is this job for you?" "What are your personal goals in life?" "How does this job complement them?" Mix in a handful of other questions, and you're shown the door with a quick smile and brisk, "We'll be in touch."

I took a breath, collected my thoughts as the elevator slowed, and straightened my back when the doors began to part.

"This way," Ms. Blackwell said.

We entered a floor that was completely different from the floor where Ms. Blackwell worked. It was beautifully decorated in masculine browns, from the walls to the furniture to the hardwood floors. There were no cubicles here. No areas where people were typing away or collaborating. In fact, as we moved through the quiet space, there appeared to be no people, period. At the tall windows were massive shades, which blocked out the daylight so the artificial lighting—strategically placed around the space—could create a more intimate, welcoming mood.

This is his floor, I thought. *He doesn't have a corner office like other executives. He has an entire*

*floor. And why not? He owns the joint. Please, don't
let him be an arrogant prick.*

Ms. Blackwell turned a corner and we came
upon an elegantly dressed young woman with blonde
hair. She was perhaps my age. Maybe a bit older.
Late twenties or so, but completely pulled together
and professional looking. She smiled up at us when
Ms. Blackwell and I stopped at her desk.

"Ann, this is Jennifer Kent. Jennifer, this is Ann
Collins, Mr. Wenn's executive assistant."

Her title surprised me, but then I figured she
must be staying on until a replacement was found for
her position.

"It's a pleasure to meet you," I said.

She stood and held out her hand with a smile.
"The pleasure is mine, Ms. Kent. It's good of you to
come. I'll let Mr. Wenn know that you're here."

She brushed past us.

"Thank you, Ann," Ms. Blackwell said, watching
her go to the only office on this floor. At least it
appeared to be an office—there was a closed door
there. The rest of the floor was a wide-open space
broken up by the sitting areas. It was unconventional,
to say the least.

Blackwell turned to look at me, and in her eyes was a sense of urgency. "The rest is in your hands. Keep a cool head and an open mind. Think 'big picture.' Think 'future.' Don't be a fool and think too much about this. And best of luck to you, Jennifer. Remember the pin in your hair. Use it at the right moment. Use it instinctively."

Without another word, she walked away, leaving me alone to wonder what she meant about not being a fool and not thinking too much about this. Why did she want me to keep an open mind, to think 'big picture' and 'future'? What did any of that mean? And why was she so focused on my hair? At that moment, I wished Lisa was with me. She'd see through the undercurrent of what wasn't being said. I was naïve in these sorts of situations, which was probably part of the reason why I hadn't scored a job in this town. People likely could smell my lack of life experience.

"Ms. Kent?"

I looked over to where Ann was standing beside an open door.

"Mr. Wenn will see you now," she said.

I smoothed my hands over my suit, checked my chignon a final time, and started to close the distance between us.

"Can I get you something to drink?" she asked before I stepped inside. "A glass of champagne? A martini?"

"It's only noon."

"Your point?" I must have had an odd expression on my face when she said that because she put her hand on my arm and laughed. "Let me get you a martini. One as smooth as silk and as cold as January. A martini never hurts anything." She stepped aside. "Please," she said, motioning toward the room beyond. "Mr. Wenn is waiting."

CHAPTER TWELVE

When I stepped into the dimly lit room, I could smell the faint scent of leather and the even fainter smell of cigar smoke, neither of which was unpleasant. In fact, the effect was almost calming.

There were no windows here, just paneled walls with paintings on them and a Tiffany lamp that cast warm florid hues sitting upon a table directly to my right. Across from me, the shadowy figure of a man moved into the light as Ann closed the door behind me.

"Mr. Wenn?" I asked.

"It's Alex," he said. His voice was deep and soothing. "I'm glad you decided to come, Jennifer, especially after your experience with Ms. Blackwell the other day. I apologize for that. I hope she was kinder to you today."

When his face came into view, time seemed to slow, and then it morphed into a shape I didn't recognize. It couldn't be him, but it was. This was the man who helped me on the street, when my briefcase was knocked out of my hand the last time I was here. This was the man who ran down the sidewalk to retrieve whatever he could of my flyaway resumes. This was the man I instantly was attracted to when I watched him walk toward me with that sheen of sweat on his chiseled face, which was covered now with the same dark stubble I remembered from two days ago. I thought he looked like the designer Tom Ford, only better.

Ms. Blackwell forced herself into my thoughts, and now I knew why her words made sense: *Keep a cool head.*

I wasn't sure if that was possible, but I nevertheless forced myself to keep a neutral expression as I extended my hand to him. "This is a surprise," I said.

He shook my hand, and when he did, his large hand engulfed mine.

"If this were a different interview with a different woman, I wouldn't have believed that. But the other day, it was obvious you didn't know who I was, not that it matters much. Still, the fact is that it doesn't happen often. In our brief moment of chaos the other day, I was a kid again. With you, I felt anonymous." He gestured around his office. "It was as if none of this is important, and it isn't. At least not to me."

I didn't know what to say, so I said nothing.

"Please," he said, letting go of my hand. "Sit with me."

He motioned toward two comfortable-looking leather chairs that faced each other in the center of the room. Side tables with low lamps sat on either side of each. I fell in step behind him, still in a haze of disbelief that this was happening. He'd seen me at my worst—frazzled, frustrated and vulnerable. He knew I'd been crying when he entered the elevator that day. He saw me walk into that man, and he knew it happened because I'd turned back to look at him.

What am I doing here?

I took one of the chairs and sank into it. It was firm, but forgiving, like a little piece of heaven. The cool leather felt good against my skin, especially when I crossed my legs and my calf pressed against the bottom of the chair. It sent a chill through me.

Or was that because of him?

I watched him sit down. He was wearing a black suit that hid a tight, muscular build hidden beneath. His cobalt blue tie set off the intensity of his blue-green eyes, which now were caught in the glow of the lamps on either side of him. He seemed to study me for a moment. With a confidence I didn't know I possessed, I did the same.

"I'll come clean," he said. "When you left the other day, I went straight to Blackwell and asked for your resume. I see that you're from Maine."

"I am."

"Do you miss it?"

I thought of my parents, and then of the few friends I'd left behind. "Parts of it."

"Which parts?"

"The good parts."

He smiled at that, and then turned when a knock came at the door. "Come in, Ann," he said.

The door opened and Ann entered with a silver tray, upon which were two glistening martinis. She seemed impossibly regal and elegant to me, which brought out insecurities I was trying to tamp down.

Watch her, I thought. *Learn from her. Look at how she moves. This is what it's like at the top. This is what he'll expect from you.*

She handed me a martini, which I put down on the table next to me. She then turned to give Alex his.

"Thank you, Ann."

With a slight nod of her head, she left the room. When the door clicked shut, he raised his glass to me. "To new possibilities," he said.

I reached for my drink, and leaned forward to touch glasses with his. We sipped and, as promised, the liquid was smooth and cold. Still, I felt like a fraud. I didn't have half the sophistication Ann had, and I was here to replace her? Give me a break.

I am so not at this level. Martinis at noon? Who does that?

The answer came at once.

Mr. Wenn does that.

I looked at him, and saw that he was watching me with a directness I found, at once, exciting and intimidating. He was beyond handsome. He looked as if he'd stepped out of the pages of *GQ*. Or off the cover.

"I noted on your resume that you have an MBA."

"I do."

"What did you hope to find when you came to Manhattan?"

"For starters? A job. So far, that's been futile."

"Why do you think that is?"

"If I knew, I'd likely have a job."

"I can't imagine why you'd have difficulty finding a job here."

I remembered what the cabbie said to me the other day, and offered it up as a possible explanation. "The economy is in the can."

"Not for someone like you. I think you might intimidate people."

Why do I keep hearing that? "How?"

He shrugged and sipped his drink, but didn't answer. "What did you hope to find at Wenn? I understand you applied for a secretarial position. Why?"

"To be blunt, I need the money. I've been here since May. Money is tight at this point, so a girl needs to work. I figured if I could get my foot in the door, someone would see that I had talents that went beyond answering phones, and then maybe I'd get a better job within the organization."

"You know, if I asked that of someone else, I would have been given a line of bullshit."

"That's not me."

"I assume that's the Mainer in you."

"Where I come from, we have ethics."

"I know you do. When my parents were alive, we had a summer home on Hancock Point. I still own it, actually, though I haven't been there in years because I've been so busy here."

"It's beautiful on the Point. You must have loved it there."

"I did. When I was a boy, I spent most of my summers in Maine. Initially, some people resented me because I was one of the summer people. But over time, that went away. The people I befriended were locals. I came to know them and I played with them, much to the chagrin of my mother, who was a snob. Through my friends, I realized how lucky and unlucky I was. I had plenty to eat, which most of my friends didn't. But my friends had lasting friendships, which I lacked because of who my family was. Maine gave me a good perspective on the world."

"How about Manhattan?"

"It's a completely different perspective. A ruthless one. I don't feel anything here. If I could retire to the country or to the coast, I would. But apparently my destiny is to carry out my father's legacy, which was decreed to me in his will without my knowledge of it." He raised his eyebrows at me. "So, there's some 'no-bullshit' information about me. I think we're even now."

As much as he had bared, I could sense it was only the tip of whatever drove him to share it with me. His voice was almost clipped when he spoke. He didn't seem happy to me, which intrigued me. This man appeared to have it all—he was a billionaire with his own building on Fifth Avenue, for God's sake—but there was an unmistakable sense of sadness about him that I'd probably never understand. His 'no-bullshit' response was telling, but only to a point. There was a mystery within him, an undercurrent of something darker that I'd likely never put my finger on. I sensed that he would go far to protect his privacy, which he should. What he gave me only was for show, though I appreciated his effort to make me feel at ease.

"I need to come clean with you, Jennifer."

That piqued my interest. Had he been lying to me? If so, about what? "How so?"

"I asked you here because I needed to make certain that you were the one."

"For the executive assistant's job, you mean?" I reached behind my head, and did what Blackwell had told me to do. I pulled out the long black pin and shook out my hair without once leaving his gaze. I felt the weight of my hair tumble down my back, but my attention remained on him. Steady and unwavering.

He watched me, finished his martini in one long swallow, and glanced away. He seemed uneasy and distracted. "I'm asked to attend a lot of social events," he said. "Several each week, most of which end up with me doing some kind of business for Wenn. There's a party tonight in fact. I don't like going to them because I end up going alone. Women try to attach themselves to me, and I know what they want. They aren't interested in me. What they want is the money and the notoriety that comes from being with me. I know that sounds arrogant, but it's nevertheless the truth, and I hate it. At any one of these events, there is not one woman there who is interested in me as a person. What they see is a bank account and a lifestyle. I'm not seeking an executive assistant, Jennifer. What I'm seeking is a beautiful woman like you who would attend these events with me and, as ridiculous as it sounds, pretend to be someone I'm seeing."

I felt my stomach sink, along with my heart. "You're asking me to be your escort?"

"If you're using the word escort in the traditional sense, then absolutely not. This isn't about sex, and I'd never insult you like that. All I'm seeking is a well-paid companion who will keep the wolves at bay so I can meet the people I need to meet, and move my business forward by striking the deals I need to strike at these sorts of events. I'm asking you to pose as my girlfriend. But it would only be an act. Yes, we'll occasionally need to hold hands for show. I might give you a peck on the cheek. There needs to be some sort of physical indication that we're a couple, but I'll only do what you agree is comfortable for you. If it's just occasionally holding hands, or me whispering in your ear, or us sharing an intimate laugh, or perhaps having a dance, then that's it. I'll never cross whatever boundaries you establish. Only you and I will know about this, but people need to believe that we are happy together and that there is chemistry between us. I already think that exists. At the end of the event, I'll take you home, we'll say our goodnights, and Ann or Ms. Blackwell will be in touch with you about the next event. Look," he said. "I know this sounds insane, but I don't feel as if I have another option. I'm not interested in dating anyone right now or for the foreseeable future. I want to focus on my work, and I want to be left alone to do it. I don't want women distracting me. I don't want to be romantically involved. It just ruins things. Does that make sense?"

"How does it ruin things?"

He didn't answer my question. "I just need to know if this makes sense to you."

"I suppose it does in a crazy sort of way." And it did. I could see why women would throw themselves at him. He was one of the best-looking men I'd ever seen. Surely, I wasn't alone in that opinion. I could see women approaching him and trying to get to him, and how that could be an unwanted interruption.

"I hope I haven't offended you," he said.

I reached behind my head and lifted my hair off my neck, which felt warm. I pulled it over my right shoulder, and it curled around my breast. "You've surprised me. I wasn't expecting this."

"I think you're beautiful, Jennifer. And you seem to be a kind person, which matters to me. I like that you're from Maine. I respond to that. If you'd consider taking the job, I'd be grateful."

"Exactly how is this going to read on a resume?"

"That you were my executive assistant. Or whatever title you'd like to choose. It doesn't matter to me. If you find this isn't for you, I can find work for you here at the same salary. No hard feelings. I'm sure there is an executive-level position that Ms. Blackwell could find or make up for you here. But I'd need you to give this a chance first."

"How long of a chance?"

"Three months."

"How many events per week?"

"It can be up to five. For the better part of each week, we'll essentially be inseparable during the evenings."

Blackwell entered my head: *Keep a cool head and an open mind. Think 'big picture.' Think 'future.' Don't be a fool and think too much about this.*

"This is strictly platonic?" I asked.

"Strictly."

"I'd prefer not to be kissed." *Because I'm afraid that if you do kiss me, I'd want more.*

"Whatever you're comfortable with."

"Holding hands is fine. A dance actually would be nice. It's been a while since I've had a dance."

"Same here."

"So, we can have a dance. And I understand the situation. We need to look intimate. You can whisper something in my ear if you want. We can hold hands, and you can place your hand on my back. But that's where it needs to end."

"Anything else?"

"That should be simple enough. I'll warn you that I'm not much of an actor."

"Neither am I. I guess we'll each have to find our way. But we do have chemistry together, Jennifer. I saw it on your face when you turned to leave the building the other day. You probably saw it on mine."

"I was too busy picking up resumes," I lied.

"If you take the job, you won't need them any longer."

Don't be a fool and think too much about this.

I looked at him, and decided to see how serious he was. "All right," I said. "I'll take the job. But the salary needs to be adjusted to three hundred thousand dollars."

He didn't flinch. "That's fine."

You've got to be kidding me? I kept my features neutral. "Perfect. When do I start?"

"Tonight," he said. "There's an event at The Four Seasons. Eight p.m."

"Tonight?" I said. "But I don't have anything to wear."

"You will soon. Ms. Blackwell is going to take care of that for you now. Get what you want. She has a good fashion sense and knows how you should dress for tonight's occasion. Tomorrow morning, you two will shop for rest of the week. All clothes and anything else you buy are yours to keep, but I need to make sure that you never wear the same thing twice."

"You're saying that to a woman as if that's a bad thing?"

"You have a point."

"I can keep the clothes?"

"And the jewelry."

"There's jewelry involved?"

He smiled at me, and as much as I knew I shouldn't react to that smile, I nevertheless felt it cut through me like a blade. He was devastatingly handsome when he smiled. But as much as I was attracted to him, I knew I had to think of him more like a brother. I could not fall for him. This was a business transaction. Period. That's how he viewed it, so that's how I needed to view it.

"There's lots of jewelry involved," he said. "My girlfriend would only have the best of everything, right?"

"I guess so."

"Ms. Blackwell will take care of that, as well."

"Am I using my own name?"

"You are. And your own story. You're from Maine—feel free to talk about that. You recently graduated with your master's in business—talk about that, too. Ms. Blackwell has all the details about how we met and got to know one another. Make sure you read them carefully and memorize them." He winked at me. "We need to have our schtick down, Jennifer. We need to make the wolves believe so I can get my work done."

CHAPTER THIRTEEN

"Well, look at you," Ms. Blackwell said. "Your hair is down. I'm assuming you took the job? Of course you did. Good for you."

I was standing outside her office, having just come from my meeting with Alex. I was in a bit of a daze, but I tried not to let it show. Blackwell, sharp as ever, nevertheless saw it.

"You'll be fine," she said. "And you have to admit, it's a sweet job. I think you'll be pleased. I've known Alex since he was a boy. He's a good man and he has a big heart, which he fiercely protects. Thus this new position for you. After all he's been through, he does not want to be involved with anyone now. It's too distracting. But he's a gentleman and he'll do right by you, Jennifer." She raised an eyebrow at me. "I assume I can call you Jennifer."

"Of course."

"For me, it always will be Ms. Blackwell."

I couldn't help a smile. *Which is likely why you're getting a divorce.* "That's fine."

She touched her hair, which was dyed black and cut in a severe, angular bob that suited her personality. "I can't exactly break my tough-as-nails reputation around here now, can I? You understand."

She stood and reached for the pair of glasses next to her computer. "I hear we're going shopping," she said. "And we don't have much time to get it done before tonight. So, where to first? Bergdorf? Tough to go wrong there. And then, I think Cartier. Some diamond studs. A beautiful ring and bracelet. And obviously a necklace. Something classic. That's what the night calls for."

"He told me I could keep everything."

"That's right. Perks. And don't forget, dear. He's a billionaire. Whatever we buy today, tomorrow and going forward is a drop in the Wenn bucket."

She grabbed a piece of paper off her desk and handed it to me. "This is how you two met. In the car, commit it to memory. It's not much, but you need to have it down. You'll wing it a lot when you're together with him tonight—I have a feeling you two will riff off each other. But what's on that piece of paper is your script. Don't ever deviate from it."

"Noted."

"There's a car waiting downstairs for us. What time is it?" She checked her watch. "Christ. It's already past one. We need to move on this. Tonight's important to him, and we are not going to disappoint."

"What is tonight, anyway?"

"Another benefit. This one to support the Met, which is one of the bigger events. It's not their gala, which is why it's at the Four Seasons, but everyone will be there, so no pressure. It's another way for him to make the sort of connections that will keep Wenn Enterprises moving forward. He never wanted the position his father put him in, but Alex always does what's right, despite how his parents treated him. He's determined to keep the company growing, but lately, that's been difficult for him. Too many women trying to catch the eye of the eligible bachelor. That's where you step in."

"So, I gathered."

"Come on, princess," Ms. Blackwell said as she moved past me. "We need a dress, shoes, undergarments, and jewels—in that order. And STAT. I don't know how we're going to fit that ass of yours into a dress without tailoring, but we'll do it. Hopefully. And, no, that wasn't an insult. It was envy. Every woman wishes she had a body like yours."

"Why don't I feel that way?"

"Seriously, Maine? Seriously? You either need to wash your mirrors, or you need to get your head checked. God! Let's go."

* * *

Outside the building, a black stretch limousine was waiting for us at the curbside, and once again, I was struck by how quickly my life was changing.

"Bergdorf," Ms. Blackwell said to the driver, who was holding open the rear door for us. "We need to step on it. *Rápidamente*!"

I sat next to her, the driver got inside, and off we went down Fifth, only to cut over to Sixth, so we could make the loop that would bring us to our destination.

"Read your notes," Blackwell said.

"I am."

"Don't miss a word."

"I don't intend to. This isn't exactly rocket science. There are only three paragraphs here."

"We made it simple for you."

I shot her a look. "You could have made it complicated, and I still would have nailed it."

"Maine," Ms. Blackwell said, stretching out the word in exasperation. "Maine, Maine, Maine. Stop being so sensitive. We made it simple because we don't want you overwhelmed on your first night. And you probably will be overwhelmed for good reason. This is a new world for you. We were just trying to be helpful. God!"

"Sorry."

"Read!"

* * *

When we arrived at Bergdorf, Ms. Blackwell was on a tear.

"Valentino," she said as we hurried through the store. "That man understands women. He celebrates curves. Or, at least, your curves. I'm a stick. But look at what he did with Sophia. No stick figure there, but an icon nevertheless. He understands how a woman should dress. If we're lucky, we'll find something, it will fit, and then we can move the hell on and find some shoes. That will be easier. Hopefully Dior because, after all, they're goddamn Dior. Then the undergarments, which must include Spanx. They will even you out nicely, but you might not be able to breathe, which doesn't matter to me and shouldn't matter to you. Consider it a concession for looking great. Then we get out of here and get to the good stuff at Cartier."

We took the elevator; Ms. Blackwell crossed her arms and tapped her foot as we rose. The doors slid open, and I followed her as she steamrolled toward the Valentino section.

"Somebody," she said to no one in particular. "I need assistance. Straight away. As in now." She snapped her fingers above her head. "Hello! We need assistance here. Stop sexting, people. And, yes, I said sexting. I know how you young people are. You can do that on your lunch break. You're probably sexting each other and you don't even know it. God!"

A young woman appeared beside us. She was model material—tall, fine bones, creamy skin, pale blonde hair. If she was annoyed by Ms. Blackwell's demands, she didn't look it. Her mouth was set in a half-smile. "How may I help you?"

"Valentino," she said. "Something black. A gown. Very pretty, very chic, very Valentino. Über, über, über." She motioned toward my butt. "And it needs to fit that."

I blushed.

The woman appraised me from behind, which was ridiculous, and said, "I think I have something. It arrived this week. It's a bit unconventional, but it's a showstopper. It's not on the floor, but I can take you to it."

"It's like we're going to a viewing," Blackwell said.

"Excuse me?"

"You know, a corpse. A viewing." Her brow furrowed. "But you don't know. You're too young to know. The idea of death means nothing to you now. But it will—just wait and see."

We followed her into a round dressing room. A pedestal was in the center of the room, surrounded by tall mirrors. One of the mirrors was a door. The woman opened it, disappeared inside for a moment, and then came out with the dress draped over her arms. "It's exquisite," she said. And then she let the bottom of the dress drop as she held it up, so we could see all of it. She slowly turned it to reveal all of it.

"It's stunning," I said.

Ms. Blackwell went over to study it. "Leather bodice. Sleeveless. Lace at the throat. A layered tulle skirt with silk lace accents. The back is gorgeous. Look at the treatment of the lace, Jennifer. Very intricate. Very pretty. Obviously hand done. Oh, Valentino. No corpse here. Divoon." Her eyes flicked up to meet mine. "What size are you?"

"Five."

She looked at the clerk. "Will this fit her?"

"It might."

"Strip," Blackwell said. "We'll put it on right here."

I'd spent enough time in a gym not to feel awkward undressing in front of two women. I removed my suit and draped it over one of the chairs behind me as I saw that Blackwell was sizing up my body. And then, with the clerk's help, I put on the dress.

"Well, it's beautiful," Blackwell said. "But it needs to be tailored. Somehow, it fits your ass, which is a goddamn miracle, but the bodice needs to be fitted. Don't you agree?"

She didn't ask me. She asked the clerk, who nodded. "I could ask our tailor to come in, and we could have this for you in a week."

"It needs to be done within the next hour," Blackwell said.

"I don't think that's possible, madam."

"How much is the dress?"

"Twelve thousand."

I felt my throat constrict.

"We'll pay twenty thousand if the tailoring is done within the hour. Can you make that happen, or do I need to speak to your manager?"

"Give me five minutes," she said, and she left me alone with Blackwell.

"Money is mute, but it always talks," Blackwell said.

"Twenty thousand dollars?" I said. "For a dress?"

"Jennifer, that's nothing. Get over it. Now, turn around. Let me see."

I did.

"Turn to your left."

I did.

"Now face me."

I faced her.

"This is the one—and on the first shot. How the hell did that happen?"

"I believe it was the clerk's idea."

"She had a vision—I'll give her that. Now, she needs to get me a tailor."

The woman did, Blackwell smiled, and the fitting began.

* * *

When we were finished, we found the perfect pair of Manolo Blahnik Bakhita double-buckle sandals with three-inch heels. I loved them on sight, and was relieved when Blackwell agreed. Next, I followed her to the undergarment section, which she happily raided. We paid for it all, and then we left the building for Cartier, where Blackwell wasted no time finding exactly what she wanted. Never once was I consulted.

"That ring," she said to the clerk. "That necklace. That bracelet. Those studs."

I tried them on, and dipped down to look at myself in a long rectangular chrome mirror. *This can't be happening*, I thought as I pressed my fingers against the diamond necklace. *This is a dream.*

"Even the ring fits," Blackwell said. "Turn to look at me."

I did as I was told.

"Those are nice, but we'll do better next time." She turned to the clerk. "We'll take them all."

By the time we left with our packages and stepped into the waiting limousine, Blackwell had dropped more than one hundred fifty thousand dollars on jewels.

"You've now got everything," she said. "We'll get ready in my office. How did it get to be so late so fast? We've got to hustle. We've only got two hours left before you're supposed to meet him."

"Where am I meeting him."

"You'll take the elevator to the forty-seventh floor at eight. He'll be there to greet you."

She pulled out her cell from her Birkin, tapped out a number, and said, "Bernie, it's Blackwell. I'm a bit stressed, but otherwise divoon, divoon, divoon. Always divoon. Look at me, I'm divoon. I'm also in a crunch. Can you help me with hair and makeup? I'll pay whatever you want. No, it's not for me. It's for a lovely young woman named Jennifer Kent. You'll be hearing a lot about her tomorrow—trust me. Yes, she's very pretty. This won't be a lot of work, but time is running out, and I need you now. Oh. I see. Well, could you cancel her appointment, love? For me? You know how well I tip. Yes, I'm sure it will inconvenience her, but Bernie, you have no idea how much I need you now. You can hear it in my voice, which is thick. I'm on the edge. Desperate. Pleading. Don't make me despondent. Perfect. You're a lifesaver. What was that? She has dark hair, newly dyed by the looks of it. No, we're not dealing with a kitchen-sink dye job with this one. It was done well—I'll give her that. Right. My office. Thirty minutes. Love, love, love."

She clicked off the cell and leaned against the leather seat. "Kent, you're killing me." She held up her hand before I could speak. "Don't apologize. Or even argue. You were thrown into a tsunami. I get it. I'm just pulling you out of it. I think Alex will be pleased, don't you?"

"I can't wait to see how it all looks together."

"It'll work. You'll see. I have an eye. Don't worry. And thank God we got Bernie. He's a magician. You won't recognize yourself when he's finished with you. He'll make certain that all other women will pale next to you when you're standing next to Alex. And that's the point, isn't it. How did Alex put it to me? Oh, yes. Keeping the wolves at bay. That's what you'll do. I have no doubt. Tonight, I see you working a smoky eye and a pouty lip, just like I used to wear when I was a kid at recess. Only that wasn't done with cosmetics. It generally was done with kicks and fists. Now, read your script."

I did, but I longed to call Lisa. When we returned to Wenn, I'd excuse myself to use the restroom and call her from one of the stalls. At this point, she likely was worried about me. I needed to reach out to her before the melee launched into full swing.

* * *

"I can't believe this," Lisa said.

I was in a restroom on the fifty-first floor. I went to the very last stall, and was relieved to find that, at least for the moment, the restroom was empty.

"Believe it."

"It's too much."

"Try being me."

"I *want* to be you!"

I spoke quietly. "I've only given you the abbreviated version because the Kraken is waiting for me. I don't know when I'll be home tonight. Don't wait up."

"I'm so waiting up. Are you sure you'll be safe?"

"I've told you where I'm going, whom I'll be with, et cetera. If anything happens to me, which I doubt, you've got the deets. Look, I better go. I've been gone too long. She's going to freak out on me. I'll see you tonight."

"Good luck!"

I clicked off the phone, actually used the restroom, washed my hands, and quickly went back to Blackwell's office.

"That took awhile," she said.

"We've been gone for hours. You can call me Niagara Falls if you'd like."

"That's unnecessary. Bernie will be here in seconds. I've secured one of the conference rooms for us. The lighting is better there, and we'll have privacy. No windows. I've asked maintenance to bring up mirrors."

"Thank you."

"It's my job, Maine." Her face softened for a moment. "But you're welcome. You've been nothing but professional today. I appreciate that."

A compliment from Blackwell? Obviously, after four long months of trying to make it in this town, I was on my way in ways that I hoped that I was prepared for. But I probably wasn't.

CHAPTER FOURTEEN

Just before eight p.m., I stood in front of a mirror, and couldn't believe the person I'd become. From the dress to the diamonds to the upswept hair and makeup, I looked like the sophisticated woman I always wanted to be, though rarely felt like. Especially after being beaten down by my father for years, and being rejected dozens of times over the past four months.

But the woman I saw now? She gave me confidence. I turned in front of the mirror, and admired the dress again. Then I looked at Blackwell, who was alone with me, as Bernie had already left.

"What do you think?" I asked.

"I think you're going to break someone's heart."

I furrowed my brow at her. "Whose?"

"Maybe your own."

"I don't understand."

"Just remember that this is a job. That's the best advice I can give you. You're playacting. Nothing more. Don't read into anything, because he won't be. You're a means to an end for him."

"You're talking about Alex?"

"Who else?"

"But we already spoke about the job. I understand the situation. It's purely professional."

"You're still young," she said. "And as bright as you are, probably a bit naïve, which is natural. If you get swept up in the moment, if he touches you and you feel yourself responding, remind yourself that this is a job. Do that, and you'll be fine because I can promise you this, Jennifer. When he's with you, Alex only will be going through the motions with you. He's a good man, but he's focused on his work right now. Work is all he has. Work is all he can handle. You're nothing more than an object to him. That sounds harsh, but it's true. On the surface, you'll make a handsome couple, people will believe it, and you'll earn your salary because of it. What will ruin this for you is if you become emotionally attached. He'll sense it in an instant, and he'll fire you for it."

"Why is work all he can handle now?"

"You just need to trust me on that."

"You make it sound as if something happened to him."

"You're reading way too much into this."

But I sensed I wasn't. There was something about him that she wasn't telling me. As cool as Blackwell was, even she couldn't hide this secret.

But what does it even matter? I thought. I need this job. She's giving me advice for a reason. Fine. As attractive as he is, I'm an object to him. That's worth over a quarter million a year, never mind the perks. I'll meet people through him. I'll make important contacts. This is just the beginning for me.

"I should go," I said to her. "It's almost eight."

She went over to a table and retrieved an elegant beaded black clutch.

"We forgot to get one of these today," she said, handing it to me. "It's mine. You can borrow it. Judith Leiber. Inside, Bernie left lipstick and I added mints. That's all you should need."

"I suppose a flask won't fit in here."

"Very funny."

"Or some Xanax."

"I did consider that...."

"But what about perfume?"

"Bernie gave you a touch. Perfume should only ever be an intimate experience. Think of it as a secret shared between you and your partner. Only he should smell it. No one else."

"But that will be Alex," I said.

"So, it will, but don't worry. He won't notice. I can promise you that."

CHAPTER FIFTEEN

I said goodbye to Blackwell, and she reminded me to be prepared to go shopping in the morning because I had another event tomorrow night. And with that, I stepped into the elevator.

It was a minute before eight, so, despite how hectic the day had been and that I was starving because I'd had nothing to eat, I had made it. Still, Blackwell got me through. Whatever my initial impression of her was, I had to hand it to her. Without her, I wouldn't be standing here now, and I certainly wouldn't be looking like this. This was by far the best I'd ever looked, and it all came down to her eye and her friendship with Bernie, who was a genius as well as an artist.

But I was nervous.

After pressing the button for the forty-seventh floor, I felt the car sink right along with my gut. What would he think? Would he be pleased with what he saw? Would I pass inspection? I couldn't afford to lose this job—especially this job. Even if I only lasted a week with him, that one paycheck would hold me over for a month. And then there were the jewels.

I'm an object, I said to myself. *That's all I am. But I'm still charming. Still sweet. Still Jennifer. To the public, we were made for each other, even if that isn't the case. That's what I need to sell.*

And that's what I intended to sell.

When the elevator slowed and the doors started to part, my heart thrummed in my ears. Alex was standing just beyond the elevator when the doors slid open. As promised, he was in black tie. He had a grin on his face, and his hands were in his pockets. He looked dashing, and I felt my heart skip a beat.

"Jennifer?" he asked.

"One order to go."

"Very funny. You look beautiful. Step out for a moment. Let me see."

I moved out of the elevator and because I was damned if I wasn't going to be myself, I twirled in front of him. "This is like an out-of-body experience for me," I said. "I never look like this."

"To me, it looks like an in-body experience. This is all you. I don't know what to say. I knew you'd be—" He stopped himself short. "I mean, there was no question...." He shook his head. "Never mind. Thank you for going to such trouble. I couldn't have asked for more. I'm going to have the prettiest woman on my arm this evening. I can't tell you what that means to me."

"You'll be able to get business done," I said.

He paused for a moment, and then nodded. "Right."

"That's what this is all about. We'll keep the wolves at bay. Do you like the dress?"

I watched his eyes soak me in. I don't think he was aware of it, but when he spoke, it came out as a low growl. It sounded like, "Very much," though I couldn't be sure.

"Ms. Blackwell and a clerk chose it for me."

"They may have chosen it, but you're the one wearing it."

"Ms. Blackwell insisted that I wear my hair up. Do you like it this way?"

"I actually like it when you wear it down, but Blackwell is right. At this sort of event, you'd wear it up. The better to see your graceful neck, not to mention the necklace. Maybe later, when I bring you home, you can take it down."

It was an odd request from a man who only saw me as an object, but maybe that object also served as a fantasy figure for him. Not that he needed it. For whatever reason, Alex said he wasn't looking for a relationship, but there still was a raw air of sexuality about him, and he had the look of a man who was enjoying his share of women on the side. Right then, looking him in the eye, there was something almost predatory about him. I wondered what his type was. I wondered how many women he slept with during a given week. No man who looked like him and who had his kind of money wasn't getting his share of it when he wanted it. I was certain of that.

This would be so much easier if I wasn't attracted to him.

"Should we go?" I asked.

"First, tell me how we met."

"Oh, that was two weeks ago. We met at MoMA. Both of us were admiring our favorites—the Impressionists. We struck up a conversation. You suggested lunch. Lunch turned into dinner. We've been inseparable since."

"Sounds romantic," he said.

"It does."

"But I like our story better. You looking back at me when you left the building. Me standing at the door looking at you. The connection we made, and then your collision with the fat man."

Why is he talking about connections? It's confusing. "I could have done without the latter."

"At least he had some padding. It could have been worse. All of that chunk of his couldn't have hurt too much."

"I think my pride was hurt the most."

"I hope today made up for it. And tonight. Are you ready for tonight? The press will be there. They'll photograph us. You need to be prepared for that. You'll be in newspapers and on blogs tomorrow. People have been waiting four years for me to find someone. And you're it, at least to them."

"Why four years?" I asked.

He shrugged, but didn't answer. Was that when his parents died? Was he in a long-term relationship and it ended four years ago? I was surprised by how little I knew about him, but I kind of liked it that way.

I enjoyed the mystery, which would protect me. The less I knew about him, the better. *He's an object. I'm an object. Keep it that way. You don't need to know anything about him.*

He reached out his hand for mine. "We probably should get used to this," he said. "You know? So we look natural together."

I took his hand in my own, and felt the heat pass between us. He pressed the button to call the elevator, but the doors immediately slid open. Obviously, no one had used it since I stepped out. We walked inside and stood silent, his shoulder against mine. The elevator plummeted to the lobby, and as we fell, he squeezed my hand.

It's too much, I thought. *I thought he'd be indifferent to our arrangement until we were in public, but he's being anything but. He knows I'm attracted to him. He mentioned our connection. Is he just playing along so I'll look all dreamy-eyed when we arrive at the Four Seasons? Maybe that's it. In fact, that is it. This is important to him. The illusion needs to be real. People will know if it isn't. He's just doing what he needs to do. He's playing me. Go with it.*

Outside, a limousine was waiting for us. The driver wasn't Eddie, but another man who stood beside the rear door, which he held open. It was warm out, but at least the sun had dipped below the Manhattan skyline. Ever the gentleman, Alex motioned for me to step inside first. I tucked my dress behind me, lowered my head, and slid across the seat, hoping that I wouldn't wrinkle the material too much on our drive to the Four Seasons. He stepped in after me, reached again for my hand, and held it on his rock-hard thigh.

"Who are you hoping to see tonight?" I asked.

"Darius Stavros. He's a Greek shipping tycoon. Wenn Oil is expanding. I'm hoping that we can come to a reasonable agreement to use his ships to export our oil."

"That will be complicated."

"He'll make it complicated."

"I know he will. It's his reputation."

He turned to me as the car pulled into traffic. "You know of him?"

"Of course, I do. I came here to use my MBA, remember? For years, I've devoured the business sections of any number of newspapers, mostly the *Times* and the *Journal*. I'm a business junky. I have to say, he seems like a son of a bitch to me. He's too old. He's off his game. I don't want to speak out of line, but if I were you, I'd go through his son, Cyrus. He's poised to take over his father's empire. I'd talk with Darius first, but just keep it to a friendly chat. I wouldn't talk business with him. If Cyrus is here tonight, I'd mention your idea to *him*, and see if he proposes anything. He's young—maybe early thirties. And he needs to leave his mark, which Darius obviously doesn't. But if Cyrus brings something to his father that has real potential to further their shipping empire, it'll be a game changer. Darius will finally see the initiative he's been waiting for years to see in his son. Do you know how powerful that is? Cyrus has a reputation for being a playboy. He's a good-looking screw-up. If he shows some interest in his father's empire and brings Darius a good deal, you're on your way because Darius will want to encourage his son, not discourage him. Not at this point. As far as I see it, if you get Cyrus, you'll get Darius. And then the negotiations will begin."

A look of surprise came over his face. *Yes, I'm more than just this dress, Alex. I worked hard in school. I came here to succeed in business, not to do this. Though this is a business deal, I guess, despite how tightly you're holding my hand.* "Do you know if Cyrus will be there?"

"He'll be there. He goes everywhere with his father now, for the very reason you just pointed out. As you said, soon his father's business will be handed down to him."

"Then go to Cyrus," I said. "He has something to prove. He's your key, and you're his."

"Jennifer," he said. The way he said it sounded as if he was about to thank me.

I squeezed his hand, and I have to admit that I felt a little powerful when I did so. The business world was in my blood. I finally felt a trace of confidence because I was talking about things I knew and loved. There was no awkwardness when it came to talking about the world to which I wanted to belong. "There's nothing to say. Feel free to use me for business advice at any point."

"But that will cost extra," he teased.

"I think I'm fairly well compensated, so no worries."

"Then why am I worried now?"

His voice was serious. "About what?"

"About this ending sooner than it should. You're very bright. You gave me an angle I didn't consider

Christina Ross

myself. I don't know why someone hasn't hired you, but they should have by now. I still think it's because you intimidate people."

"I'm a small-town girl from Maine. Before today, I was pretty much down to my last dime. How could I intimidate anyone here?"

"With your beauty," he said. "And your intelligence. For whatever reason, you don't see it. But others do. Why don't you see it?"

I wasn't going there with him, so I was relieved when the car started to slow. I looked through the windshield. "Looks like we're here," I said.

"You didn't answer my question."

"I don't intend to. I have my reasons, but they're private. This is a business relationship. I need you to respect that."

"I apologize."

"There's no need to."

"Are you nervous?"

"Not anymore. Now that I know why we're here, I'm excited. Work your magic on Cyrus. I'll work mine in other ways."

"What ways?"

"You'll see."

"One thing," he said.

"Yes?"

"I always come to these events alone. I meant what I said earlier—your presence with me will cause a commotion. Just hold on to my hand, and get ready for the press. It will be intense, they'll shout out questions, but we say nothing. OK?"

The driver opened the door. Flashes of light started to go off, and I leaned toward his ear, a sign of intimacy that was part of our agreement. "OK," I whispered. "I say nothing."

And the melee began.

CHAPTER SIXTEEN

When I stepped out of the car, the driver held out his hand to me. He assisted me with my dress so I wouldn't step on it and take a digger on the sidewalk, so, because of him, I made a graceful exit despite the fact that I couldn't see anything due the blinding explosions of light.

Alex was right behind me, which fueled the crowd of reporters more when they realized that we were together. I reached out my hand to him. He lifted it to his lips and kissed it, and I felt my knees go weak at the touch of his soft lips and the stubble on his chin against my skin.

That stubble is going to get me every time, I thought.

Deal with it.

In front of everyone, with that sort of lingering kiss on the back of my hand, he had just marked me as his own. No one knew about our arrangement. But with that simple gesture—which broke the rule of no kissing—the news would quickly spread that, at least on some level, Alexander Wenn was taken.

The questions began in earnest, but Alex just smiled and nodded to the crowd before leading me toward a line of other men and women in evening wear who were walking past the doorman and through the door he held open for us.

There was a staircase to our left. With his hand still firmly holding mine, we moved up the stairs to the receiving area. I'd heard so much about this iconic institution, I took it all in as if I might never see it again.

At the top of the stairs would be the Grille Room, as well as the bar. Down a hallway to the left would be the famed Pool Room where deals were struck every day over lunch. How often had I read about this place? About how important this restaurant was to the business community? I couldn't believe I was here. The warm light glowed deep, and had the effect of making everyone look younger than they were, which likely was intentional.

I could hear a buzz of activity coming from the Pool Room. And then there was society itself. Most were talking in small groups, enjoying the glasses of champagne being offered on silver trays by the attractive wait staff. Others stood at the bar; this group was comprised only of men sipping glasses of Scotch with other men. Not one woman was part of that group, which said it all to me, and which disappointed me. This still was a man's world into which I'd likely never fully enter. If I was lucky, I'd be tolerated along the periphery, but that's where it would end.

As I looked around, I noted that the women in particular seemed adrift in ether, their shoes barely touching the floor. I was relieved to see that I wasn't overdressed.

Blackwell nailed it.

So, this is what it's like to be rich, I thought. *And powerful. And successful. It's incredible.*

"Champagne, Mr. Wenn?" a server asked.

Alex picked up two bubbling flutes and handed one to me. "Thank you," he said to the young man, who nodded before stepping away. Alex touched his glass against mine, we sipped, and I watched him admire me over the rim of his glass. I couldn't tell what was an act and what was real. All I could remember was our arrangement, though I sensed there was something else between us. Or maybe I just hoped that there was. He turned me on physically and intellectually, a rare combination if ever there was one. I returned his smile, and then felt his hand press against the small of my back, which I permitted.

"I'm searching for Cyrus," I said quietly to him.

"He's likely in the Pool Room with his father. Darius likes to hold court there."

"When do you want to spend time with him?"

"Later," he said. "I know most everyone here, so I'll need to say my hellos. I want to introduce you to those who will approach us—which will be everyone—but I need to keep things moving quickly, so I don't lose Darius or Cyrus to the night. These events can go by quickly. Too quickly. I need to be careful of that."

"You've got a second set of eyes in me."

"What I have are many eyes on you. Unless you haven't noticed, Ms. Kent, you're the buzz of the ball. Or whatever this event is."

"It's a fundraiser for the Met."

He sipped his champagne and smiled at me. "Oh, that's right. Sorry. The Met."

Could his eyes set me on fire any more than they already did? I couldn't let them or him get to me, but that was a lost cause.

"And so it begins," he murmured to me. "Here comes Tootie Staunton-Miller and her husband, Addison, or Addy. She's difficult, but he's a very nice man, probably because he's in a sham of a marriage and knows it." He checked himself. "Actually, that's not fair. I like Addy regardless of his secrets. He's one of the kinder people you'll meet here tonight."

I watched an elegant couple move toward us.

"What do you mean about Addy?"

"He's gay. It's notorious, but no one speaks of it. You'll like him. Everyone likes him. As for her? Not so much. They have their own arrangement. I suppose lots of people here do."

He looked up at them as they approached. "Tootie," he said. "So good to see you." He gave her a peck on each cheek, and then held out his hand to Addy, who shook it.

"Hellohoware?" Tootie said, glancing sideways at me. "It's been what? A week? You look very handsome, Alex. But, then, you always do. Who is this?"

"This is Jennifer Kent," he said.

She nodded at me. "Hellohoware? Are you of the Philadelphia Kents?"

"No. I'm of the Maine Kents."

Tootie, who was fiftyish, though her face had been molded and pulled into something that stretched toward fortyish, smiled tightly at me. She had blonde hair that just touched her shoulders, and wore understated jewels at her throat, wrists and fingers, and a light yellow gown that I had to admit was sublime. I knew next to nothing about fashion, but in her form-fitting dress, which could betray more mature curves, Tootie Staunton-Miller looked trim and terrific. She also reeked of class and old money.

"I don't know the Maine Kents," she said. "Should I?"

"I doubt it."

"Oh." She looked at Alex with confusion, likely because his hand was still on my back and it appeared to those not in the know that we were a couple.

"Are you of the Northeast Harbor set?"

"No."

"The Seal Harbor set?"

"Sorry."

"The Grindstone Neck set?"

"Not even close."

"The Bar Harbor set?"

"I'm not."

"Which set are you from?"

"I don't have a set. Unless Bangor is a set."

She lifted her eyes to the ceiling and seemed to breathe a sigh of relief. "Of course. So sorry. I always think *coast*. I always think *Atlantic* and *rocky shores* when it comes to Maine. When the lumber barons ruled Bangor, there absolutely was a set, which has roots in Philadelphia and New York. I'm assuming that's your set."

"I'm afraid it isn't."

"Oh, dear."

"It's a pleasure to meet you, Ms. Kent," Addison Miller interrupted. He took my hand in his, and kissed the back of it. That was twice tonight that someone had made such a gesture. Maybe Alex hadn't crossed the 'no kissing' line. Maybe this was just who they were. The first one I received was from a stud who now was stroking my back, and the second one was from a gay man who had a gentle demeanor I immediately liked. I couldn't imagine a better combination for my entree to society, but then I loved gay men.

"It's a pleasure. Please call me Jennifer."

"Jennifer it is. You look lovely, my dear. Ravishing."

"Thank you, Mr. Miller."

"It's Addy. Always Addy. None of this 'Mr. Miller' stuff."

He really was kind. Better yet, unaffected, unlike his wife.

"Is that Valentino?" Tootie asked.

"It is."

"I saw it on the runway."

"You don't say?"

"Paris. That leather bodice will certainly turn heads tonight."

"I would imagine the designer intended for that."

"It seems so aggressive for an event such as this. Leather and lace to support the Met. Goodness!"

"I think it's beautiful," Alex said.

"Hear, hear," Addy said.

Tootie blinked at Alex. "Oh. Well, of course, it is. Valentino and everything. You can't go wrong. Well, not really."

"I can't imagine anyone judging him," Alex said. "As you know, my mother wore him often. She loved his work. You remember mother in Valentino, don't you, Tootie?"

"What I remember is her in Dior. But, yes, also Valentino. And Karl, of course. She loved Karl. Such style your mother had. Such panache. Did she ever go wrong? No. Fashion was just an extension of her. We miss her so much, Alex. Even after all these years."

"Thank you, Tootie."

"Are you two seeing each other?"

The question was so abrupt, I blushed, wondering how Alex would handle it.

"We are. It's only been a few weeks, but we are committed to each other, and we're very happy."

"This is cause for celebration," Addy said. "It's been too long. I'm happy for each of you."

What's been too long?

"So am I," Tootie said, though her voice was so cool, it was clear that she didn't mean it. I wasn't part of any set she could relate to. I was common in her eyes, which was fine by me because it was true. I was common. I had nothing on these people. I didn't belong to this group, and I didn't want to belong to it.

The one part of me that Alex never would take away was my sense of self, though there was every chance that he could steal my heart—if he wanted to. I might have been wildly attracted to him, but I would stick to the limited script he set out for me to memorize. However, in my soul, I always would be Jennifer Kent, the poor girl who had the bum parents, and who struggled to make it through college, and who was struggling to make it now in New York. That's who I was, and I wasn't about to change that person for anyone. I'd rather give all of this up and be a server shucking pricy food in a New York restaurant than be untrue to whom I was. So, at least for now, Tootie would just have to deal with me, as I sensed others would have to tonight.

"It's great to see you two," Alex said. "We should probably mix. It appears that everyone is here tonight."

Tootie leaned forward, and kissed Alex her on the cheek. I saw her whisper something in his ear as she did so, which caused him to gently pull back, his face an expressionless mask.

"Have a fine evening, Tootie," he said. He looked at Addy, whose face wore a concerned look. "It's always good to see you, Addy. You're one of the few here with genuine class. It's so rare to find. I'm always happy to see you."

"And I'm always on your side, Alex."

"I know you are." And with a devastating look at Tootie Staunton-Miller, whose face had the look of a woman who had gone too far, Alex pressed his hand against my back, we said our farewells, and we moved deeper into the room.

CHAPTER SEVENTEEN

For the next hour, it was more of the same, and I'd be lying if I said it wasn't daunting. As we made our way toward the Pool Room, where Alex believed Darius Stavros would be holding court with his son Cyrus, Alex introduced me to dozens of people I'd either read about or heard about, and each time he told someone that we were a couple, I needed to remind myself of Blackwell's advice.

If you get swept up in the moment, if he touches you and you feel yourself responding, remind yourself that this is a job. Do that, and you'll be fine because I can promise you this, Jennifer. When he's with you, Alex only will be going through the motions with you. He's a good man, but he's focused on his work right now. Work is all he has. Work is all he can handle. You're nothing more than an object to him. That sounds harsh, but it's true. On the surface, you'll make a handsome couple, people will believe it, and you'll earn your salary because of it. What will ruin this for you is if you become emotionally attached. He'll sense it in an instant, and he'll fire you for it.

I had to think of him as though he was my brother. I considered that angle during the interview, but now I needed to embrace it. It was the only way I was going to get through this. My attraction to him was that great. And, frankly, I needed the job.

As we walked through the crowd, everyone who came our way seemed interesting until they opened their mouths.

People complimented me on my dress, my hair, my lovely shoes, my jewels. But once they realized I wasn't one of them, no one asked anything meaningful about me. To them, I also was an object, a bit of arm candy for Alex, and even though I could sense their surprise when Alex said that we were seeing each other, I still felt like vapor. Most looked straight through me. I was a meaningless nobody at worst, a curiosity at best, and someone to gossip about later.

But I remained professional. If the conversation turned toward business, which it often did, I tossed in a bomb of surprise and spoke with confidence and knowledge about whatever topic was being discussed. In some cases, that earned me a confused look from the men, a second glance from the women, and sometimes a leading question to see if I really knew what I was talking about, which I did. Mostly, Alex kept the conversation light and pressed on, only to meet more people he knew.

And the process repeated itself.

Much of it was like a series of interviews, and the undercurrent was clear—how could I possibly have landed Alexander Wenn, of all people, especially when I wasn't one of *his* people?

The questions were routine.

Where did you two meet? Oh, at an art exhibit— how nice. What is your background? Oh, how charming—you have your MBA. And how unusual. Do you plan to use it? You do? Goodness! Where do you call home? Maine? How lovely. We summer there. Where do you winter?

When it occurred to them that Alex might be attracted to me because I had a mind, a look of consternation came over their faces. It was then that I saw the sexist limitations still inherent in their society. Men were the thinkers and doers, and with few exceptions, women apparently were meant to be glittering bobble heads.

It was as fascinating to me as it was insulting. For the most part, women were expected to smile and nod while the men spoke about such masculine, difficult subjects as business. When the women were called upon to speak, they admired each other's dresses, they spoke of their families, whatever rigorous renovations they were undertaking at any number of their homes, and what part of the world they were off to next. Obviously, I knew nothing about society or its rules, but I was damned if I was going to be the pretty village idiot.

Later, when we moved farther down the hallway that led to the Pool Room, Alex squeezed my hand and asked if I was having a good time.

"It's an interesting crowd," I said carefully.

He laughed at that. "I love how you're making them squirm. None of them knows what to make of you."

I looked at him. "Sorry," I said. "I can't help myself."

"Why should you? I want you to be yourself. Look. They're either of a different era, or of a different upbringing. Or both. Most of the people here are in the book. You know about the book? I thought so. Very little has changed in their circles. This is exactly why I loved my time in Maine. I was surrounded by real people. The women I came to know through my friends were strong-willed and smart." He shot me a sidelong glance. "Not unlike you."

"I can't play dumb," I said.

"I don't expect you to. And by the way, most of the women here went to Smith or Vassar. They're just playing the game. They come to these events first as packages of elegant subservience designed to bolster their husbands' careers, and second as a women who are able to talk airily about absolutely nothing of substance. I'm used to that. You're not. And I can tell that it's wearing on you, which I get. Do you want some advice?"

"Please."

"Keep screwing with them. Play the game, but do it for your own entertainment. I don't care because I know that you won't insult them. When they talk about visiting Bora Bora, tell them that you found

Mount Merapi in Indonesia more interesting, and that you'd go back to the Celebes Sea in a minute. Their eyes will cross."

"Have you been to those places?"

"Awhile ago."

"Did you climb Mount Merapi?"

"I did. At night."

"But that's an active volcano."

"So, it is."

"Are you some kind of jock?"

"I used to be. Now, I just like to work out. It's a good distraction."

From what?

Talking to him alone put me at ease. I was starting to understand how he worked this crowd. He put on a show for them, they put on a show for him. Apparently, that's how it worked.

"Shit," he said.

"What's the problem?"

"Just do your best. Red dress. Black hair. Coming our way."

"One of the wolves?"

"She could be a pack of them. Be ready for her. She won't be kind to you. She'll try to slay you." He paused and put his hand even more firmly against my back. "Immaculata," he said as the woman stopped in the middle of the hallway to stare at us. "How are you?"

She was gorgeous—tall and statuesque, but older than Alex and me. Probably late thirties, but I wouldn't have been surprised if she was in her early forties, regardless of how beautiful she was. It was tough to tell. She looked at me, absorbed me, and then she turned to Alex with betrayal in her eyes. "Alex," she said. "What a surprise. I thought you said you were coming alone tonight?"

"That was last week."

"Oh, last week. Last week. You make it seem so long ago. You make it sound like it was years ago, but it was only last week. Seven days ago. Just seven days since we last spoke."

"Things have changed since then."

"What things? Why haven't I heard? I hear everything. People call me. What could have changed in a week?"

Alex was about to speak, when she turned to me. "Who is this?"

"This is Jennifer Kent. Jennifer, this is Immaculata Almendarez."

Who in the hell has a name like that?

When she finally closed the distance between us, I extended my hand, which she took lightly in a dismissive way before dropping it.

"It's nice to meet you, Immaculata."

She raised an eyebrow at me. "Isn't it?" She put her hand between her formidable breasts and laughed. "Just joking. Please, don't look so serious. It's just my sense of humor. It's a pleasure to meet you, too, Jennifer. Cute dress. What are you doing with Alex?"

This broad held nothing back. I was beginning to see why Alex needed me here. He had to get to Darius Stavros before he left. If I wasn't here, I had no doubt that she'd hold him up and he'd miss that opportunity.

Before I could answer, Alex intervened in an effort to shut her down. "We're seeing each other, Immaculata. I hope you'll be happy for us."

"You're what?"

"Seeing each other. Just over two weeks now."

"Which means you were seeing each other last week?"

"We hadn't made it public yet."

"I see. How mysterious. How smoke-and-mirrors of you. Where did you meet?"

"At MoMA."

"How romantic. You met over art. Probably mooning over one of the pastels. Did you just strike up a conversation?"

"We did. Over the Impressionists."

"You don't say?" She turned to me with venom in her eyes. "And here I thought Alex and I had a connection. I feel so silly right now. I came here alone tonight because I thought he was coming alone. So much can change in a week. Or two weeks. Who's counting? Is that Valentino?"

"It is."

"A gift from Alex?"

I wasn't going to let her get the best of me, so I went there. "It was. Along with the jewels. Don't you love them? He chose them specifically for me. He's so good to me." I leaned over and kissed Alex on the cheek, and thereby broke my own rules. When I kissed him, I smelled the faintest scent of his cologne. It coursed through me because it was masculine and understated, just like he was. When I pulled away, I sensed his surprise, especially when I began to rub off the lipstick I had left on his stubbled cheek with the back of my thumb. "Thank you again, darling. No more lipstick. You're good."

He looked at me in such a way that wasn't unwelcoming. "It was my pleasure," he said.

"Anything that comes from Alex is a pleasure. I can only imagine how pleased you are with his gifts and with him."

"You have no idea, especially when we're alone. What do you do, Immaculata?"

"I go to parties. I attend events. I sit on boards. I don't work because I don't have to. Work is a four-letter word to me. Yourself?"

"I work."

"Oh, my dear, that's like saying 'fuck.' Not that I say that word often. But it's true. It's like saying 'fuck.' Who works?"

"I work in business and I love it."

She pressed her hand to her chest and laughed again. "That's so unusual."

"Why is that?"

"None of my female friends work. I just find it unusual, that's all. They also would."

"It's probably just your generation."

"It's probably just my what?"

"Your generation. I'm twenty-five. When it comes to my generation, we can't imagine not being creative or contributing something to the greater good."

"I think I need a martini."

"Servers are swarming, Immaculata. Just keep your eye out for one. Are you a Gibson girl?"

"Am I a what?"

"A Gibson girl."

"I don't know what that is."

"It's a cinematic reference."

"Why can't I understand you?"

"It's not important."

"Who do you work for? If you're with Alex, I'm assuming a Fortune Five of some sort."

"Not at all. I work for myself. I'm a consultant."

"A consultant! And an entrepreneur. At twenty-five. So impressive, Jane."

"Jennifer."

"Jennifer. My mistake. On what do you consult?"

"Business."

"Of course, you do. Why didn't I think of that?"

"Because it's a natural extension of working in business?"

"I wouldn't know."

"Why would you? All those parties to manage. It must be dizzying."

"I have an assistant."

"Someone once said that a managed life is an unstructured life. Or something like that." I felt spears of hatred coming in my direction when I said, "Your dress also is cute. Who are you wearing?"

"Darling, at this point, I've lost count. Somebody somebody. I'm sure they're very successful and in all the right magazines. All that matters in life is beauty."

"I wonder what the people in some third-world countries would feel about that? Or the homeless in our own city?"

"The what?"

"The homeless."

"I don't know them."

"It's never too late to educate. As for me, my vote for what matters most in life would be love and relationships. Never beauty. That wouldn't be first."

"So, I see."

I touched a hand to my necklace, and the ring on my finger glinted in the light. I smiled at her.

"Well," Alex said. "It was good seeing you, Immaculata."

"Just good? You're leaving?"

"We have business to attend to," I said.

"Business, business, business. Since when are you all about business, Alex? I used to talk to you for hours at events such as these. Business sounds so boring. Business sounds like Ambien to me."

"It sounds like what?" I asked.

"Like Ambien."

"I don't know what that is."

"It assists with sleep."

"Oh, a sleeping pill. Like the ones Michael Jackson took?"

"I'm sorry?"

"He died from some sleep-inducing methods. I assume Ambien was involved."

"This has nothing to do with that. Or with him."

"I hope not."

"Ambien is very well known."

"I haven't heard of it, but I sleep well at night. My conscience is clear. I just drift away in seconds, unless Alex has other ideas. Anyway, to us, business is exhilarating. It's what gets us up in the morning. And it's probably one of the reasons we fell in love. We have something in common that we adore.

Actually, many things. I think we complement each other well."

"I'm sure you do."

"Good night, Immaculata," I said. "It was swell meeting you."

"Swell?"

Before I could respond, Alex said good evening to her, and we moved forward.

"What was that?" he asked quietly.

"The end of Immaculata. Isn't that what you wanted?"

I could sense him trying to suppress a laugh. "Yes. I just didn't know you had that in you. Who are you, Jennifer Kent?"

Apparently, I continued to surprise.

CHAPTER EIGHTEEN

We entered the Pool Room, which was more impressive than the photographs I'd seen of it. The pool was in the center of the room. It was square and glowed with bubbling light, and lovely, fully grown trees were along its periphery.

I spotted Darius Stavros almost at once.

I leaned toward Alex's ear. "Stavros is with a group of people at two o'clock. Cyrus is behind them looking bored."

A photograph was taken of us before I could pull away.

"We'll be seeing that somewhere tomorrow," he said. "Shall we go over and say hello?"

"Why not?"

"I'm going with your plan."

"I hope it works."

"I think it will."

"Look at him. As good looking as he is, Cyrus is a shadow in his father's limelight. He needs that plan."

"That's twice you've said that he's good looking."

"He is. He's got that Greek thing going on. It works for him."

And why do you care if I find him good looking? You've been kind, Alex, but I'm your employee. I'm just here to keep the wolves at bay.

"But back on topic," I said. "He has to give his father something substantial soon, or even more disappointment will settle in. I have to say that as wealthy and as irresponsible as he is, I kind of feel for him. He's the heir to everything his father built, yet he might not want to be part of it. From what I understand, Darius has no other sons. Because of that, he might be forcing his business on Cyrus. So, let's help him out. Let's give him something to hand to his father. Something sweet. Something he can feel good about."

He looked as if he was about to say something, but checked himself. He seemed conflicted to me.

Was it something I said? I wasn't sure. It occurred to me that he might need to believe in the illusion we had created, and I may have broke it when I commented on Cyrus' looks. He had, after all, just called me out on it. I wouldn't do it again.

"You've noticed that—with the exception of Immaculata, whom you shut down—I haven't been bothered tonight, haven't you?"

"I've noticed. I've also noticed a few angry women along the sidelines. Daggers have been fired at me. Knives and cannon balls."

"Which means this is working. Thank you for that."

"My pleasure. And thank you for the job."

"I hope it doesn't feel like a job to you."

There was a new note to his voice that I couldn't define. *Why do I feel as if this is sliding in the wrong direction? Keep it light.* "Look at me. I'm all dolled up. This is fun." I nodded across the room. "Darius is parting company. Now's your chance to say hello."

And Alex did.

After a few minutes of introductions and conversation, in which Alex only talked family with Darius, he turned and looked in surprise at Cyrus, who was standing behind him.

"Cyrus," he said. "I'm sorry. I didn't see you."

"How are you, Alex?"

"I'm fine. And I'm happy to see you. This is Jennifer Kent."

Cyrus looked at me longingly and openly, leaving no doubt that on some level, he found me attractive. "I've been watching you since I first saw you," he said. "I think you noticed. Or I hope you did. Sorry, Alex. I couldn't keep my eyes off her. You're lovely, Ms. Kent."

For whatever reason, Alex's hand tightened around my own. It wasn't just a squeeze. It felt possessive. There was a definite shift in the air. "We recently began seeing each other."

"Congratulations. I can see why. A friend of mine, Constantine, also noticed you, Ms. Kent. I have a feeling he and I are not alone."

"Cyrus," Alex said, "I have a proposition for you."

"But I was just admiring Ms. Kent, Alex. Why take the spotlight off her so quickly? I have a feeling most of the men here tonight are also admiring her. Where are you from, Jennifer? If I might call you Jennifer."

"Jennifer is fine, Cyrus. I'm from Maine."

"Maine. It's beautiful there. Of course Maine would produce you. It makes sense, don't you agree, Alex? Only Maine would produce this kind of raw beauty."

Was he serious? Who talked like that?

"If we could talk about the proposition...."

"You mean the proposition you have for my father?"

"No, actually I have one for you. Would you care to hear it? I think it might interest you."

A server came up beside me, interrupting the conversation. I looked at him. "Yes?"

"I have two drinks for you, madam."

"From whom?"

"Two gentlemen admirers. I believe they'll introduce themselves to you later."

I looked at Alex, who looked annoyed. "One glass of champagne is enough for me," I said.

"You should indulge," Cyrus said. "You're obviously a hit here tonight. You're a new face. And a stunning one. Sorry, Alex, but it's true. I've been watching the men watch her. We need someone like Jennifer here tonight—she's made it more interesting. Everybody else knows one another. I have a feeling that people don't know that she's with you. I certainly didn't earlier because I was planning on approaching her myself. Is this serious?"

"Very."

The server looked confused. "Should I take away the drinks, madam?"

"Yes. And please thank whoever sent them. But I never have more than one drink, so I'm afraid I'll need to pass."

"She's also with me," Alex said. "I expect you to tell them that."

The server nodded and walked away.

"That sounded territorial," Cyrus said. "But I don't blame you. If she were with me, I'd do the same thing."

"About the proposition," Alex said.

"Of course. I'd like to hear it. Will Jennifer come? I assume she knows about it."

Again, Alex's hand, this time just above my ass.

"If you'd like. I think Jennifer would be happy to come."

Cyrus looked at me, his eyes drifting away from mine and down to my breasts. He was good looking, sure, but also an absolute creep. "I would like."

For reasons I didn't understand, Alex looked as if he was seething. He was getting his audience with

Cyrus, which is what he wanted. I was supposed to be nothing but an object to him. That was the arrangement. Why would he care if others were paying attention to me? Why the sudden change in mood? I didn't get it.

"Then let's talk," he said.

CHAPTER NINETEEN

As Alex planted the seed of his idea, Cyrus seemed less interested in it than he did in me. Alex made his pitch, but Cyrus kept stealing glances at me, which I thought was rude. This time, it was *my* hand that went to the small of Alex's back, which stiffened when I touched it. Instinctively, I pulled back. What was his problem?

"So, you need our ships?" Cyrus said when Alex was finished.

"In a mutually beneficial relationship, yes."

"Are you able to send me a formal proposal? I'd like to show it to my father. He will need to be involved in this, though I'm happy that you came to me first. I appreciate it."

"You'll have a formal proposal tomorrow. It's clear to all of us that one day you'll take over for your father. Out of respect for that, I wanted to come to you first."

"That was kind of you." Cyrus turned to me, his gaze lingering once more on my breasts. Despite how indecent he was being, I kept my expression interested and polite in an effort to help Alex. "What do you think of the deal, Jennifer? Should we take it?"

"I don't think I'm qualified to answer," I said.

He turned to Alex. "Is she qualified?"

"She's more than qualified."

"Do you mind if I hear her opinion?"

"If you'd like. Of course."

There was a coldness to his voice that I didn't understand, but my job here was to assist him, so I did. I cocked my head to the side so Cyrus would lift his eyes to meet mine. When they did, I went in for the kill. "I see it as win-win. Wenn Oil is an industry leader. So is Stavros Shipping. I recently read that you increased your fleet of ships substantially when you took over a significant portion of Anastassios Fondaras' shipping company. I think you know the report I'm referring to."

"The one in the *Journal*?"

"That's right."

"Not all of that is true."

"Probably not—journalists always tend to get some details wrong. But if you do have several ships sitting empty due to the economy, here's an option. And from where I stand, it's a solid one. Wenn Oil has a steady supply of petroleum it must distribute. You have the means to make that happen. Come together on a fair price, and I think everyone will be pleased." I paused for a moment, and then I smiled at him. "I think your father would be impressed that it was you who nailed this down. Alex could go to any number of industry people he knows—he has the world at his disposal—but he didn't. He told me tonight that he wanted to work with you. He made that very clear. It's why we came tonight."

"It was?"

"It was. Alex said that was his goal. I assume the fact that it was he who came to you about the deal will remain private. Just between you two."

"It would," Alex said. "As far as I'm concerned, this is your deal to propose, Cyrus. You're the one who thought of it, not me."

"Wenn Oil is a catch," I said. "Your father knows that. This could be a significant deal if negotiations go well, assuming they go forward at all. I guess that depends on you and your father, and on how you respond to the proposal."

"And here you thought you weren't qualified to talk on the topic. You're very bright, Jennifer. Looking the way you do, I wouldn't have expected that."

Sexist motherfucker. "I hope I didn't speak out of turn."

"Of course not. I asked your opinion. I just didn't realize it would be so informed."

I was insulted, but I didn't let it show. Instead, I smiled. "Business is in my blood. It's one of the reasons I'm with Alex. Finally, someone I can talk to who gets it."

"I wonder who else you could talk to who gets it?"

He didn't allow me a chance to respond.

"I'm eager to see the proposal," Cyrus said. "Will you email it directly to me, Alex? There's no need to CC my father."

"Of course."

"Tomorrow afternoon?"

"You'll have it by noon."

"And I'll be in touch, hopefully sooner than later. I appreciate that you thought of me first. Or was that Jennifer's idea?"

"It was Alex's," I answered.

"Jennifer is right," Alex said. "We've known each other for years, Cyrus. You were at the top of my list. Of course, I'd come to you first."

"Others would have gone to my father. We'll work something out. I'll make sure of it."

"Thank you, Cyrus."

"We'll talk tomorrow." He turned to me. "And it was nice meeting you, Jennifer. A pleasure. Alex is a lucky man."

"I know I am, Cyrus," Alex said. "Until tomorrow." He reached for my hand, and we walked into the crowd.

CHAPTER TWENTY

With Alex's hand firmly holding mine, we stepped away from Cyrus, past the bubbling pool, up a set of stairs, and down the hallway that led to the Grille Room—and the exit beyond.

People tried to stop and talk to Alex along the way, but he only offered them a curt nod and a smile, which was unlike him.

Given the briskness with which he walked, the night obviously was over. Our mission was accomplished. There was no question in my mind that Cyrus would respond positively to Alex's proposal. But right now there was a clear undercurrent that Alex was unhappy with me.

I glanced at him, and saw that his face was set. Expressionless. He looked like a different person to me. Whatever warmth and humor he had shown to me earlier was now gone.

What did I do wrong? Did it really matter to him that I told him that I thought Cyrus was good looking? Was that it? Or that men ordered me drinks? Or that Cyrus wouldn't stop coming on to me? It didn't make sense to me. Why would that matter to him? I was an object to him. That's what we agreed upon. Again, the only thing I could imagine is that by saying that I thought Cyrus was attractive, I'd broken the illusion that we were a couple. Nothing else that had happened was in my control. It seemed absurd to me that he'd react so strongly to my faux pas and to Cyrus' advances when he had clearly noted that this was a business arrangement. I might be wrong, but my gut said differently.

Ahead of us, an orchestra was playing in the Grille Room. When we arrived earlier, there was no orchestra or dancing. But now, far ahead of us, I could see people waltzing as their heads dipped and lifted to the music.

Coming toward us was a server with flutes of champagne on a silver tray. I tried to slow our pace to take one of the glasses because I was thirsty, but Alex was having none of it. He urged me forward and we walked past the man. To our right were the stairs that would lead out of the building and down to the street. This night was over with an exclamation point. Somehow, I'd blown it. Apparently, for whatever reason, this was it for Wenn Enterprises and me.

"Alex," I said.

He turned to me with steel in his eyes. "Would you like to dance with me?" he asked.

I was startled by the question. I thought for certain we were leaving. When I didn't immediately respond, he said, "Today, you said that it had been a long time since you danced. I'd like to dance with you. Would you consider that?"

We stopped beside the staircase.

"Are you angry with me?"

"I'm asking if you'd like to dance. It was part of our agreement. You said that a dance was permissible. I'd like to have that dance."

"I haven't danced in years. I don't want to embarrass you."

"You're quick on your feet. You just proved that. All you need to do is follow me."

He was looking at me with an intensity that burned. The offer to dance wasn't a question. It was a deal breaker if I declined.

"Of course. I'd love to dance with you," I said.

"Then let's do it."

He led me to the dance floor where we moved into the swirling crowd. He put his right hand in the middle of my back, lifted my right hand with his left, pulled me close to him, and we began to waltz.

Only this was no ordinary waltz.

Alex took charge at once and began to aggressively twirl me to the point that it was dizzying. People cleared the way for us, and others along the sidelines gathered to watch as Alex led me across the dance floor in fluid steps that were so quick and precise, I needed to put my full trust in him in order to keep up, look elegant, and make certain that I didn't make a fool of us.

For whatever reason, he was challenging me. If I stumbled, he'd make a fool of me. I didn't know why he was doing this, but he was, and I was damned if he was going to best me. When I was young and my mother was sober, she made sure I had years of dance lessons, which she herself enjoyed as a child.

What I remembered about the waltz was that to fully succeed at it, I needed to give myself over to my partner, which I did now. I leaned into Alex, turned about the floor with him, and dropped my head back as he spun me around and around and around while the crowd began to engage with interest. I made two missteps, which I secretly cursed, but when he went for the throwaway, I was prepared for it. I stretched my left leg back as far as I could, and he reached his right leg behind him in a similar fashion. We paused for a dramatic, romantic moment with our faces turned away from each other, and then he scooped me into his arms again, and we completed the dance to a rush of applause.

Alex took my hand. He bowed while I curtsied. I heard people call out his name, and then, with a pissed off look on his face, he started to leave the floor just as the orchestra started up again, this time to a slower waltz.

I pulled him back to me.

"We're not finished yet," I said to him.

"Yes, we are."

I put my arms around him, and gave him no choice but to dance. Too many people were watching us for him to leave now. He saw it, and knew it. Our bodies again became one. We started to move. I looked up at him, and saw a mixture of emotions on his face that I couldn't read.

"What's the problem?" I asked.

"I don't have a problem."

"You just tried to make a fool of me, and you lost. I may have come from nothing, Alex, but that doesn't mean I don't know how to waltz. My mother made sure of that."

"Apparently, there's nothing you can't do."

"What the hell does that mean?"

He didn't answer."

"Why would you want to sabotage me like that?" I asked.

"Don't be dramatic."

And then, without a trace of irony on his face, he looked me in the eyes and dipped me dramatically. The move was so aggressive and it hurt my arm so much, I nearly fell, but I was able to right myself before I went down. He lifted me back up.

"What the hell was that?" I said in his ear. "You hurt me. What's your problem? Be a man about it. What's the issue?"

"I didn't mean to hurt you."

"Well, you did. You just hurt my arm."

"I thought we were together tonight."

"We have a business arrangement. By all accounts, we are together. A moment ago, everyone in this room thought we were the happiest couple on Earth."

"Including the ones who sent you drinks?"

"And that's my fault?"

"And Cyrus, who obviously would take you home tonight if you let him?

"That's his issue, not mine. I never once engaged him. I deflected every compliment that came my way."

"If we were a couple, you never would have said that you found Cyrus attractive."

I tried to keep my voice low. "I'm sorry, but we are not a couple. You're my employer. Today, we came to an agreement, which I have stuck to. And then there's Blackwell. Blackwell told me to remove myself emotionally from you. She said I'd only ever be an object to you. She warned me against you."

"She did what?"

"Ask her. And by the way, Alex, Cyrus *is* attractive, at least physically. Otherwise, I find him risible. I couldn't stand his eyes on me. Good luck to him. He's a fucking creep. And he sure as hell isn't my type."

"What is your type?"

"Why does it matter? Why don't we just leave?"

"Because we're mid-song. You wanted this dance, so we finish it. What's your type?"

If I didn't stay, I'd lose a day's worth of pay that I couldn't afford to lose. After buying the Prada suit and the shoes I wore to my interview with him, I needed that money more than ever, even if the pay was just under a thousand dollars. A thousand dollars was a lot to me. It would help keep my own wolves at bay. So, we danced.

"I asked you a question."

"Does it really matter?"

"Why are you being so hostile?"

"I could ask the same of you. You wanted to make a laughingstock out of me on this floor, but you failed."

"The dance isn't over yet."

"What the hell does that mean? If you try anything with me, I swear to God I'll trip us both up. Both of us will go down. I'll make certain of that, Alex."

"I wouldn't do that."

I leaned close to his ear. "Really? Because you don't tell me what to do. What's worse is that you knew exactly what you were doing to me during our last dance, but you came up empty. Sorry about that—someone had to lose, and that was you. And by the way, Alex, yes, I know you have a lot of money—obviously—but do you really think that means shit to me? Because if you do, I'm here to tell you it doesn't. If you think it does, then you truly know nothing about Maine or its people, who you claim to know because you spent a few summers there and mingled with the commoners. You know—people like me. How nice for you. How humbling that must have been for you. Too bad you didn't learn from it."

He turned me around, but I went right back to his ear. "Here's the deal. It's not about the money for us. It's about the relationships. I could walk back to Cyrus right now, charm the pants off him, and pocket his money for a good year or more. But that's not going to happen for two reasons. First, I respect myself. Second, he's not the one for me. I've never been in a relationship with anyone. That's *by choice*, and it's for a good reason. I'm waiting for a gentleman. Rich or poor, doesn't matter. At some point, I'll find him. And I'll be happy when that happens because money won't define us. Money just ruins things. You'd be different without money. Do you know that? I don't think you do. After what you just pulled, I'm no longer interested in this job, so I'm declining it now."

The song ended.

I stepped away from him, heard him fall in line behind me, but I didn't care. I was finished. I discreetly walked to the rear of the room, where I let down my hair, and shook it out. I then removed the necklace, the ring, the bracelet and the earrings, and handed them to him. "Keep your jewels," I said. "I don't want them, or the dress or the shoes. But you will pay me for today because my time is worth something. I also helped to seal a deal for you, but I won't ask for a cut of that, even though I damned well earned it. Consider it my gift to you. I left Blackwell's clutch in your car. Make sure you return it to her. You'll have the dress and the shoes back tomorrow."

"Why are you doing this?"

"Are you serious? I've had enough abuse in my life. No man will ever treat me the way you just did."

"What do you mean you've had enough abuse?"

"What the hell do you care? Just stay away from me."

I walked past him.

"Jennifer."

How was I going to get home? I had no money for a cab, and there was no way I could walk home at night looking like this. Anything could happen to me if I did. I looked around the room, and saw the bar ahead of me. Once again, it was surrounded by men—no women. Whatever. I went over to it. Two older men parted for me, and I leaned toward the bartender. "I need to use your phone."

"Alex," one of the men said. "Good to see you."

"Jennifer."

The bartender handed me a cordless phone. I tried to remember the number to Lisa's cell. I left my own cell at home. Whenever I called her, I just selected her name from my list of contacts. I couldn't remember the last time I actually dialed her number. What was her damned number? Why was I drawing a blank?

"Please turn around."

"Those are a lot of diamonds you're holding, Alex. If the young lady doesn't want them, I know my wife certainly would."

The man laughed.

I heard the tinkling of jewels being passed behind me. "Please give these to her for me."

"Alex, I was only joking."

"They're a gift. I don't need them, Jon. Really, it's fine. It's my pleasure."

The man at my left was staring intently at me. He was older, probably late sixties and he had a kind face. I couldn't remember Lisa's number for the life of me. I turned to him.

"What do you need?" he asked.

He could sense I was in distress. I couldn't believe I was going to ask a complete stranger for money, but I was desperate. "I left my clutch in somebody's car. I need cab fare, but I have no money to get home."

He reached into his jacket pocket, removed a money clip thick with bills, and lowered it into his lap so no one could see. He peeled off one of the bills and said, "Will this be enough?"

I looked down. It was a hundred dollar bill. My eyes filled with tears when I looked up at him. "I'm so sorry to have asked, but I'm also so grateful to you. You don't know what this means to me."

He pressed the bill into my hand. "I'm much older than you," he said. "These things happen. We all are young once. Go home and be safe. Maybe this will work itself out."

"Thank you."

I turned, and saw that Alex was standing directly behind me, but knew that he'd try nothing here. Not with these men. I brushed past him and moved toward the exit, hoping he wouldn't follow, but naturally, he did.

"Jennifer," he said.

"I told you to stay away from me."

I picked up my dress and hurried down the stairs. I needed to get out of here. I went across the lobby to the door, hearing his footfalls behind me, and walked outside when one of the men standing beside the door held it open for me.

"Just give me a moment to explain."

What was the point? He just revealed himself to me. I wasn't giving him anything. I stepped onto the sidewalk and looked up the narrow street for a cab. There were none here, but there would be on Park Avenue, so I moved in that direction. Alex stepped beside me and kept pace with me.

"You don't need to do this. I know I made a mistake. Let me take you home. We can talk about it in the car. I just got jealous. I don't understand what came over me. I apologize."

I turned to him. "Jealous of what?"

"That you found him attractive. That he and other men found you attractive. That men ordered you drinks."

"What am I missing here? I was made to look like this for a reason. I'm being paid to be your escort. That's it. You and Blackwell told me that's all this was. I've been nothing but professional. I kept that dragon Immaculata at bay to help you. I also helped you with Cyrus. I gave you that angle. Fine, I said I thought that Cyrus was attractive, but who cares? And why should you care? You told me you had no time for a relationship when we first met. You said you wanted to focus on your work, and be left alone to do it. You said you didn't women to distract you. You said you didn't want to be romantically involved. Do you remember saying any of that? Am I just imagining that conversation? No, I'm not. I was hired to keep the wolves at bay, which I did. I was hired to make sure you could do your work, which you did. The arrangement was clear to me. One comment out of my mouth, a few drinks delivered to me, and suddenly you're pissed off and determined to embarrass me in front of everyone. Well, it didn't work, Alex. You intentionally hurt my arm. You wanted to hurt me, you succeeded, and now I no longer work for you. Good night."

"Give me another chance. I wasn't prepared for this. I wasn't prepared for you."

What the hell does that mean? I decided I didn't care, and looked around for a cab.

There was one coming down Park. I signaled for it, the driver saw me, and he pulled to the curb. *Thank God.*

As quickly as I could, I hurried over to it, swung open the back door, and stepped carefully inside so I didn't ruin his overpriced dress. As I shut the door behind me, I told the driver to go.

I didn't look, but I knew Alex was standing on the sidewalk watching me leave. Had I done the right thing by throwing away this job? Absolutely. I was nobody's property. I would not be treated like that or taken advantage like that by anyone. I'd learned plenty from my shitty past with my parents. And long ago, I promised myself that if anyone treated me with the sort of disrespect Alex just exhibited, I would have nothing to do with him. I couldn't do that to myself again.

"Where to?" the driver asked.

I gave him my address, rolled down the window, and let the sounds of the city and the warm breeze fall over me. Tomorrow, I'd return his dress and his shoes to him. Then, I'd look for a job as a server at one of the city's better restaurants, and wash myself of this situation.

CHAPTER TWENTY-ONE

When I returned home, Lisa was waiting up for me. She was on the sofa's foldout mattress reading a book on her Kindle, and had a martini on the table beside her.

She turned to look at me when I stepped into the apartment. "What are you doing here? It's still early. I thought you'd be late."

"I also thought I'd be late. Let's just say I was wrong about a lot of things." I kicked off my shoes at the door and watched her slide out of bed with a concerned look on her face.

"Are you all right?"

"No."

"What happened?"

"I need a drink."

"Do you want a martini? I'm having one."

"Absolutely. Three olives. Make it cold and make it dirty."

"I know how you like it. I just wish we had better vodka."

I pressed my hand on her shoulder. "One day, we will. Let me get out of this dress that doesn't belong to me, and we'll talk."

"This doesn't sound good."

"It isn't."

"Jennifer, whatever it is, I'm sorry."

"It will be fine. Sure, I gave up a well-paying job tonight, let alone the glittering diamond perks that came with it, which I gave back to him, but I actually learned a lot in the process. You of all people know how my parents treated me, especially my father. I left Maine because I refused to let them abuse me again. And guess what? Tonight was a test. Tonight, I stuck to my promise to never let anyone treat me like shit again. You know what's better? I'll be able to sleep tonight, and tomorrow night, and all the nights going forward because none of what happened tonight comes down to me. It's all on him. Screw him."

I went into my bedroom, which at this point should have been Lisa's bedroom, and changed into a pair of shorts and a tank top. As carefully as I could, I draped the dress over the bedroom's lone chair. Then I met Lisa outside the bedroom door. She had a martini in her hand and a worried look on her face. She was my family. She always would be. I gave her a kiss on the cheek, thanked her for always being there for me, and then took a long swallow of my drink.

"God, that's harsh."

"It's crap vodka, but that's all we can afford."

"Doesn't matter. It also feels good."

"Really cold crap vodka can have that effect under the right circumstances."

"Let's never forget that," I said, raising my glass. "Here's to cold crap vodka we barely can afford. You have a reason in life."

"Hear, hear," Lisa said.

I took another sip, and let the vodka sink into me. It was a hellish kind of heaven, if only because the vodka was so brutal that it burned my throat. But it was better than nothing, and it did its job. I was happy to have it.

"So, what happened tonight?" Lisa asked.

I told her everything. When I was finished, I looked at her. "Did I do the right thing, or did I overreact?"

"You said he hurt your arm?"

"He did."

"Intentionally?"

"To be honest? I don't know."

"Are you sure he tried to trip you up during the waltz?"

"If I hadn't been able to keep up with him, I would have gone down. He knew that. I'd say it was intentional."

"Well, this is complicated."

"He was a bastard on that dance floor."

"And he smoked a big blunt of jealousy before he got on that dance floor. What did you say he said about not being prepared for you?"

"Just that. He said something about giving him another chance. He said he wasn't prepared for this or for me."

"Maybe he wasn't. Jennifer, you don't see yourself the way others see you. I've told you that for years. You still see the person your parents wanted you to see. But what everyone else sees is a stunning, incredibly smart woman. A beautiful and kind person who happens to be super intelligent when it comes to all things business. You said you gave him advice about how to get to this Darius guy?"

"I did. I told him to go through his son."

"How did you know to tell him that?"

"Because anyone who reads the business pages knows that Cyrus is poised to take over his family's company, but few have much confidence that's he'll succeed at it. If I were Cyrus, I'd be feeling that lack of confidence. I'd be feeling my father's disappointment at my core. He needs to show his father something. He needs to bring him a deal. He was the logical one to approach because his father wants to see some initiative on this part."

"And Alex hadn't consider that angle?"

"No."

"Since you were hired only to be an escort, do you think it's fair to say that you surprised him?"

"Probably. He suggested as much. But who cares? I went in fully aware of the situation. So did he, as he's the one who set the rules. At the interview, Alex himself told me he didn't want anything romantic in his life right now, which is why he was searching for someone like me. He said he didn't have time for anyone. Blackwell said that I'd only ever be an object to him. That's all I thought about tonight—I was an object. She warned me away from him, probably because she could tell that I was attracted to him. Yes, I said that I thought Cyrus was good looking, but was that crossing a line given the situation? And am I responsible for the drinks that were sent my way? What am I missing here?"

"The element of surprise can be a powerful thing. Alex was prepared for you to look beautiful tonight, but he had no idea just *how* beautiful or, frankly, just how intelligent you are. There's no way he was prepared to see in action just how smart you are, or that, on the fly, you could map out a way for him to land a potentially lucrative deal. You're the complete package. I have to agree. He probably was unaware of it, and threatened by it."

"Why threatened?"

"What if someone else got to you first? What if he lost you to Cyrus? Or to those men who sent you drinks? It obviously bothered him that you found Cyrus attractive. That's when he turned into an ass." She shrugged. "But who can figure men out? I can't. I know zombies, not billionaires. But I think I'm on the right course."

"I gave him back the jewels," I said. "The dress and the shoes go back to Blackwell in the morning. I said I expected to be paid for today because I don't work for free. I plan on looking for a server's position in the morning." I took a sip of my martini, which was a necessary bit of heaven, and looked at Lisa over the rim. "So, give it to me. Did I do the right thing?"

"You and I both know why you've never been in a relationship. You saw something in him tonight that made you run. If you think you did the right thing, you know you have my support."

"That's a careful answer."

"I think this is more complicated than you realize. I think he reacted stupidly and hurtfully, and he's probably kicking himself over it now. That's why he chased after you. I don't think it's over between you yet. You'll either hear from him or from Blackwell."

"Let them call. I won't be mistreated like that. It reminded me of my father. I won't let it happen again." I held up my drink. "Actually, that's naïve. It will happen again—of course it will happen again—and when it does, I'll walk again."

"Jennifer, I just want you to be prepared for what's coming."

"What's that?"

"By standing up to him, by quitting your job, by giving back the jewels, the dress, and the shoes, and by leaving him tonight, I think you created an avalanche that's going to crash behind you in ways that you're not even aware of."

"What does that mean?"

"Nobody says no to a billionaire," she said. "You'll see."

CHAPTER TWENTY-TWO

By five the next morning, I was up and showered, the dress and the shoes were carefully packed in a box, and I had a twenty-four-hour courier service on the way to deliver them back to Blackwell at Wenn.

The cost of the service was more expensive than I had hoped it would be, but I had money left over from the cab fare the older gentleman had given me the night before, so I was good. And as there was no way I was going to deliver the box myself, this was the only way to go.

Lisa woke just after six, and I put on a pot of coffee for her. We said our good mornings, and I thanked her for listening to me the night before. She asked why I was up so early.

"The dress and the shoes are going back. A courier is on the way to deliver them to Blackwell."

"You're wasting no time."

"I want this behind me. I need a job. Hopefully I'll have one by the end of the day. Or maybe tomorrow. I have a few places lined up, and I plan on putting on the Prada and the pumps to see if I can get into one of the better restaurants. Maybe something will work out."

"I don't see you having any issues. I think you'll land something."

The buzzer sounded.

"Courier." I grabbed the box off the kitchen counter. "I'll be back in a minute."

"Do you need money?"

"Got it covered. Thank you!"

I shut the door behind me and hurried down the four flights of stairs. It was still too early to be hot, though the humidity was rising, which was somehow worse. I rounded the corner, walked over to the door, and opened it to face Blackwell herself.

Surprised, I just stared at her.

"What are you doing to me, Maine? Seriously? It's six o'clock and I'm standing in one of the worst parts of the city."

"Sorry about that, Blackwell. Some of us have to live here. Be grateful that you don't." I handed her the box. "The dress and the shoes are inside. I thought you were the courier I hired. I don't have the garment bag the dress came in, but you'll find that it's protected. Hopefully, you can take it and the shoes back."

"You've worn the shoes—the heels will be scuffed. The dress was fitted to your body. We own them now."

"Just a drop in the Wenn bucket, right? Maybe a nice girl in the office who has a similar figure to mine might like to have the dress and the shoes. Because I don't want either of them."

"Maine," she said. "Nobody has what you're packing. Nobody comes close to having your body. Don't you get it? You might as well just keep these."

"So, it's all about my body? I take offense to that. What about my mind? I lynched a deal for him last night. I gave him that idea and I made it happen."

"I understand that."

"Then give me the credit I deserve."

"Alex knows what you did for him."

"Does he? Really? He certainly didn't show it."

"He does."

"Then it came too late. He physically hurt me and he tried to humiliate me. I will not be treated like that—ever. He can screw himself."

"What happened between you two last night? I've only heard one side of the story."

So, she'd even consider hearing my side of it? That set me back. But I wasn't going to answer, because I was finished with this.

"Look," she said. "Alex wanted to come himself. I told him not to. We talked for an hour last night. I told you, I've known him since he was a boy. He thinks of me as an aunt. I asked him to let me speak to you first. In person. No phone calls. Just you and me with no promises between us. Just a talk. What do you say?"

"I've resigned from the position, Ms. Blackwell. There's nothing to say."

"I think there is. I think there's been a misunderstanding. So does Alex."

How many times in my life had I heard from my father that whatever he'd done to me the day or night before was just the result of a misunderstanding? That it was just a mistake? That things had gotten out of hand, and that he was sorry for hitting me? Too many times. And it never got better. In fact, it only got worse. The same would be true with Alex, who obviously had issues.

"There was no misunderstanding. Alex was rude to me last night in ways that I never will accept. Well, that's not true. Actually, Alex was beyond rude. He turned into a bastard. He hurt my arm, he publicly tried to make me look like a fool, and I won't have that in my life. At least not if I can help it. I may have no money, Ms. Blackwell, but what I do have is priceless. I have self-respect; I know how people should be treated, and I won't let anyone treat me like that. I'm sure others would put up with Alex's behavior because of his money, but I'm not one of them."

"So I've noted. I know you gave back the jewels."

"I did."

"And I respect that, Jennifer. More than you know."

"Great. What I do expect is a check for my time yesterday."

"You'll be paid—I'll see to it." She motioned behind her, where a black limousine was waiting along the curbside. "Just give me an hour. We'll drive around the city and talk. I have Starbucks and donuts waiting in the car for us. How can you go wrong?" Her face softened. "You know, if I didn't think there was a very good reason for me to be here, I wouldn't be here. I could have told Alex to just drop it. I could have let him come on his own, and things probably would have gotten worse. But I didn't. There's a reason for that. Please, come with me so we can talk about it."

I nodded at the box in her hands.

"I'm sorry, but there's nothing to say." I started to close the door. "You'll be fine, Ms. Blackwell. You won't have any trouble finding someone else to hold on to your boss' arm, and she'll likely give you a far easier time than I have. You know—like Immaculata. You should contact her. She'd jump at the chance."

"Alex said he'd never find anyone else like you."

"Alex was right. Have a good day."

CHAPTER TWENTY-THREE

When I returned to the apartment, I went immediately for my cell and canceled the courier. At this point, I needed to save whatever money I could. I was in luck. I was able to cancel the service and keep my sixty dollars, which, at that point in my life, was a blessing.

Lisa was having her coffee, but she wasn't in bed, which was folded back into a sofa. Instead, she was seated in the chair next to the open window that overlooked the street. As I came into the room, I knew she'd heard everything.

"So?" I asked.

"He obviously doesn't want to let you go."

"Why should he? I got him Stavros Shipping."

She blew on her coffee and nodded at me before she sipped.

"What's on your mind?" I asked as I sat on the sofa and curled my legs beneath me.

"Like I said last night, this is just the start. I write about people for a living. Specifically, people running from zombies. But that could be a metaphor for anything. I think I know human behavior and motivation fairly well. Alex is a billionaire, which gives him a leg up on other men. I bet he hasn't heard the word 'no' that often in his life, and he doesn't know how to process it. He probably can't believe that you actually denied him the privilege of being with you. And I mean that. It is a privilege. That is one man who is going to be back in your life before you know it, Jennifer."

"Let him try. I'll shut him down just as I shut Blackwell down. When I was standing down there listening to her talk about misunderstandings, all I could think of were all the times my father came to me for forgiveness. Whatever he did to me was a 'misunderstanding.' Give me fucking break."

"Sometimes, misunderstandings are genuine."

"Sometimes, they are. And sometimes I think you're taking Alex's side on this."

"That's not the case, but as your best friend who has been through a lot with you, I will say this—what happened between you and your father happened between you and your father, not between you and Alexander Wenn. Not everyone is your father, Jennifer. I understand why you have trust issues—why the hell wouldn't you at this point in your life? But what I'd hate to see is you defining every aspect of your life now by what happened to you in the past and the actions of a different person. Yes, of course, use your past to inform your present. Just don't use it as an excuse to close every door because it's easier that way. People are going to fail you repeatedly in life. Sometimes, it will be intentional. If it is, get rid of them as quickly as possible. But if it isn't intentional, or if they just did something stupid in the heat of the moment and acted up? Then hopefully you will remember that none of us is perfect, and sometimes you need to think about giving people a second chance."

"That's how you feel about Alex?"

"I don't know Alex. I only know what you told me. I couldn't sleep last night. I thought a lot about the situation, and I think what he did was childish. Do I think it was done out of malice? That's for you to answer."

"I have answered it."

"Then you've moved on, so it doesn't matter. Jennifer, I'm trying to give you some good advice. I'm talking about your future, not necessarily your present. People will hurt you—even good, imperfect people. It's unavoidable, and it's not always malicious. The good ones will genuinely regret what they did. Should you just throw them away if they screw up? It depends on what they did. But if they were good to you in the past or if you have a solid history together, I at least hope that you'd hear them out. Maybe your relationship will deepen because of it. But if you do give them that chance and they blow it again? That's when you consider closing the door and moving on for good."

"I couldn't sleep last night either."

"I heard you tossing and turning. I imagine last night was difficult for you. I laid out here wishing you could fall asleep, but I knew better. What you went through yesterday was a lot for anyone to handle—and I'm talking about the whole day. But you're still hot right now. As you begin to cool off, expect to feel conflicted about your decision. Don't say it won't happen, because it will. I believe you told me that you've never been as attracted to anyone as you were to Alex."

"That's true."

"Then be prepared for it."

In the kitchen, my cell rang. I looked at Jennifer, and said, "That didn't take long." I went over to check the screen. "Wenn Enterprises."

"That's him, not Blackwell. Blackwell had her chance."

"I'm not answering it."

"At some point, you're going to have to because this is only going to escalate. You'll see. I'm telling you, he's not going to go away."

"Then I'll deal with it later."

The phone stopped ringing, a minute passed, and the phone dinged alerting me that the caller had left a voicemail.

"Do I really want to hear this?"

She shrugged at me.

I picked up the phone, looked at the voicemail and considered playing it, but then I deleted it. I put the phone back on the counter, and without looking at Lisa, who probably thought I was insane right then, walked into the bedroom to press my suit and to get ready for the day. I needed a job to pay for that suit, not to mention the shoes. Or my rent. Or the food I needed to buy so I could eat. I had to pick myself up and get back to it, only with a different plan. I'd become a server by night, and I'd look for better jobs during the day. That would be my focus.

Only, it wasn't. As I was about to find out, Alexander Wenn planned to make certain of that.

BOOK TWO

CHAPTER TWENTY-FOUR

Over the next several days—and ironically with the help of my MBA—luck finally struck. My mood soared, even though Alex was relentless in his phone calls, none of which I answered. Eventually, he'd lay off. I just needed to wait him out and forget him, no matter how strong my initial attraction to him was.

After interviewing for a dozen server positions at top restaurants—none of which I got—I interviewed to be the assistant manager at db Bistro Moderne, an exclusive restaurant owned by the renowned chef, Daniel Boulud.

Boulud himself was in town so he interviewed me along with the general manager, Stephen Row. Each was warm and charming. We got along famously, and I got the job on the strength of my interview, particularly on the part when Boulud asked me how I saw the position.

"The first priority is customer satisfaction," I said. "It always is, as is ensuring professional service. The second is assisting Mr. Row. I imagine that I would help to oversee the front of the house floor staff, float during service time, and make certain that the staff is abiding by the restaurant's policies and procedures. This is why I received my MBA—to manage effectively and efficiently. I'm ready for that."

I heard back from them a few days later, and I got the job. The salary was more than generous, as was the benefits package. It was a far cry from the money Alex had offered me—not to mention the perks—but I couldn't have been happier. I could more than live off my wages. I could pay my bills— including those for my anxiety-inducing Prada suit and shoes—which was huge for me. And with this sort of high-profile management experience under my belt, better jobs would follow and all of those closed doors I met for months might finally be open to me one day.

The restaurant was located at Fifty-Five West Forty-Fourth Street, which was hardly within walking distance to our apartment, but given that I now had a bit of disposable money, taking a cab wasn't an issue. During our first few days working together, Stephen was helpful, but thankfully, he wasn't a micromanager. He was a handsome man in his mid-thirties with a shock of blond hair and hazel eyes framed with green flecks along the circumference. He was a true professional, and what he expected from me was simple: manage the staff, assist him when he needed to lean on me, and also—what I found really thrilling about the job—use my eye to help keep the restaurant on trend.

"Obviously, we'll leave the food to Mr. Boulud," Stephen said. "But you have style, Jennifer, and you're very bright. At this point, that's clear to all of us. You look and dress impeccably. You're also young and, if I might say, all of the staff agrees that you are stunning, which is a bonus. You're exactly who we need to spot where the city is going next, not where the city is stuck now. One night each week—a work night—I want you to take a friend and go to the city's newest hot spots. Eat a variety of foods. Put it on your corporate card."

"I have a corporate card?"

He handed me a Visa Signature Card, which I knew was one of the most difficult cards to get from Visa because the credit limit was so high. The card was in my name. I felt a thrill.

"You do now," he said. "And don't go cheap."

"How could I with this card?"

"We don't expect you to buy diamonds with it, Jennifer."

"A girl can dream."

He smiled at me. "Try as many dishes as you can stomach. Just taste them, savor them, and then move on to the next dish. I can get you into any restaurant you want, so let me know what you're hearing and where you want to go. I might make my own suggestions. We'll see. Either way, I'll make sure you get a good table. Then I need you to report back to me the next day on what the experience was like. That's how we keep ahead of the competition. That's how we trump it."

It was a dream job. And finally, I could treat Lisa, which was important to me. She'd listened to my tragic romantic woes for far too long at this point and put up with my lack of cash for months. Now, I could shower her with a night out with drinks and good food once every week, which was perfect because she was a total foodie and would appreciate it. She also would likely offer her own take on the quality. When I went home with the card and told her of my new perks, she hugged me. "I'm so subscribing to the *Times* online right now, so I can check out the food columns. We are going to get fat!"

"Oh, no, we aren't. Unless your zombies can chew the fat off us."

"I can make that happen."

After a good week on the job, I had the rhythm down. Stephen and I worked intuitively together, and we enjoyed each other, which was key. The servers were polite and professional—watching them work so seamlessly within such a narrow space only built my respect and admiration for what they did. Good service was not easy. But when it seemed easy and when the food was great, as it was here, the guests generally had a superb experience.

After so long in New York, I finally felt as if I belonged somewhere, and not just any somewhere because I knew that my job was coveted. I felt blessed and happy. And in two days, Lisa and I would go out to dinner at one of the city's hot new restaurants that was drawing raves from the press. I told Stephen that I'd like to begin at a new restaurant called Blue. He'd read about in the *Times*, and he made it happen.

"How did you do that?" I asked. "They must have been booked weeks in advance."

"Actually, months. But don't worry about it. Wherever you need to get into, just let me know. I can even get you and your girlfriend into the city's best clubs on your nights off."

"You can?"

"Mmm-hmm. It's my pleasure. And I can't wait to hear what Blue is doing. Try as much food as you can, even if it's only a few bites, then order more and report back."

Was I in heaven? Apparently I was. Blue focused on seafood, which Lisa and I both loved.

"Have fun," Stephen said. "I want to hear about atmosphere, quality of service, quality of food and drink, what their best selections look like—all of it."

"Thank you, Stephen."

"Don't thank me," he said with a grin. "You're the one who's going to gain ten pounds this month. Better join a gym."

"Can I put that on my card?"

"We'll see how you look in a few weeks."

When the night came, Lisa and I were beyond excited. In our apartment, which now had one mother of an air conditioner in the living room window thanks to an online shopping trip on Amazon, we raced about in the cool air in an effort to get ready.

"When was the last time you and I went anywhere?" she asked.

I was in the bathroom putting on makeup. "You mean beyond the laundromat?"

"Right! I mean a real girls' night out."

"Oh, that was about four months ago. I remember it well. Burger King. Just before we entered into Manhattan. We'd driven all night from Maine. We pulled over because we needed to use the restroom and because we were starving, and we each scarfed down a Whopper and fries at a particularly sticky table. Not that we really cared."

"I think we even splurged on something that appeared to be frozen."

"I believe we did. I also believe that tonight will be better."

"No frozen fish sticks for us."

"What are you wearing?"

"Something hot. You?"

"Something hotter."

"Oh, please. I'm wearing zombie chic."

"Well, then."

"By the way, I finished the third draft of the book today—it should be ready for you to read in a couple of weeks. I need to let it sit for a bit, then do the final edits, then it's yours."

"We are so celebrating tonight. Congratulations. I can't wait to read it."

"Thanks! This book practically killed me, so naturally I bought myself a killer new dress to celebrate. I'm sure my zombie peeps love fish and want me to look good eating it. Or anything undercooked. Look at me. Behold my beauty. Stand down and drink it in."

She stepped into the bathroom's doorway. She was wearing the perfect little black dress that only she could wear because she was so tiny. Her blonde hair was pulled away from her face and hung straight down her back. "You look beautiful."

"What about hot?"

"You look hot."

"Right? I mean, this kind of hotness doesn't come around just every day."

"Truth."

"Are you almost finished?"

"I just need to blow out my hair and change. Fifteen minutes."

In the kitchen, my cell rang.

"Don't answer it," I said. I turned on the hairdryer and started to dry my hair. What I wouldn't tell Lisa was that a part of me wanted to answer it. I was starting to second-guess leaving Alex that night. The further I removed myself from what happened, the more I wondered if I'd overreacted. There was no question that he went too far, but did his actions warrant shutting him out of my life and not communicating with him? I was conflicted about that, specifically because he had hurt me—physically and emotionally. I wondered what he had to say, but I still deleted every voicemail. That was reactionary on my part. That night, he had reminded me of my father and his treatment of me. But still I thought of Alex. Still, I fantasized about him. I'd been attracted to a couple of guys in college, but I never did anything about it for too many reasons I'd yet to fully face. But Alex? Alex's looks cut me to the core. So did his initial kindness when he ran out onto the street and helped me to retrieve my resumes. That was impulsive on his part. He'd been a gentleman. Was that the real him? I wasn't sure. I might have made a mistake with him, but so be it. For whatever reason, he became an ass that night. That I couldn't ignore.

I finished in the bathroom and changed into a short red dress for the evening. It wasn't new. It was something I'd had for a few years and it hadn't been expensive, but I still loved it. When I showed Lisa what I was wearing, she gleamed at me.

"I've always loved that dress."

"It's so old," I said.

"Really? Because when it comes to Blue, they've never seen it. To everyone there, it's new."

"I love you, Lisa."

"I love you more. Now let's go eat and drink. We deserve a martini with proper vodka. I might need three."

"I guess we can do whatever we want. That's expected of me. I just need to be sober enough to give them a full report tomorrow."

"I'll help you in the morning," she said. "I'm a starving artist. If this is a weekly thing, I am so helping you out."

I grasped her hand as we left. "Thank you," I said.

"For what?"

"You know what. Don't pretend that you don't. I think the world of you and I'm grateful for you."

"Girlfriends," she said as we left the apartment. "There's nothing like them."

CHAPTER TWENTY-FIVE

It was at the close of my eleventh day on the job that I left the restaurant to find a gleaming stretch limousine just outside. I didn't think much about it because db Bistro attracted that kind of clientele, and also because two hotels were on either side of me. But when I went to the curb to hail a cab and the limo nudged toward me, I knew what was up even before the rear window receded and I saw his face.

Alex.

He stepped out of the car and onto the sidewalk, and I was damned if my heart didn't race. He wore faded jeans that left little to the imagination and a white shirt that fit loosely against his muscular chest. Not that that mattered. I still could see his body, regardless of how loose his shirt was. Nothing could hide how muscular he was. On his feet were sandals.

I'd never seen him look so casual. I loved how he looked in a suit, but this was different. He looked beyond sexy and, even now, it was impossible for me not to respond physically to him. He was the manifestation of everything I found attractive in a man.

Lisa promised this was coming at some point, and here it was.

He walked toward me. "Jennifer," he said.

I was grateful that I was able to wear what I wanted at work so long as it was on trend and professional. Tonight, my hair was down, I wore a pair of off-white Dior pants I had scored for a bargain at Century 21, my blouse was red Givenchy, and my shoes were matching red Prada slingback pumps, also purchased at Century 21. Physically, I felt that I looked better than the last time he saw me, which was something of a feat given all Blackwell and Bernie had done for me, but it nevertheless was true. I had a good job and I was happy, which gave me the confidence I'd been lacking since I had arrived in Manhattan. When I nodded at him, I knew that confidence was reflected in my eyes.

"Alex."

"It's good to see you."

"How did you know to find me here?"

"I had you followed the other night."

"So, now you're stalking me?"

"I've called you dozens of times, Jennifer. I've left you at least the same amount of messages. Because you won't respond to them, I took the next step. I wanted to see you in person."

"I should leave."

"Will you give me a moment?"

"What's the point?"

"Why haven't you responded to my messages?"

"Because I don't listen to your messages. I delete them."

He looked at me in surprise, and I could sense his disappointment.

For a moment, we just stood there on the sidewalk. People walked through the silence that stretched between us as if there wasn't a concrete wall there, but there was because I had built it.

"I really should be going," I said. "I've had a long day."

"Why won't you listen to me? Or talk to me?"

I pointed my finger at him. "When someone treats me the way you treated me, they don't deserve me or my time. Leave me alone. Stop calling. I'm in a great spot right now, and I'm not interested in you. I've moved on."

He stepped closer to me. "I don't believe that."

I stood my ground and didn't move. "You should."

"I can't get you out of my head."

"There are pills for that."

"Please don't be like that. Don't be glib. I didn't come here lightly. I only came because it was clear you weren't going to return my calls. When my wife died four years ago, I never thought I'd find anyone who could stand in her shoes. But then I met you."

I blinked at him. He had a wife? She died? I felt horrible.

"I'm sorry," I said. "I had no idea."

"You're two completely different women, but even after all these years, I can feel her. This will make no sense to you, but I think she's the one pressing me to follow through with this."

"How did she die?"

"Car accident. She was on her cell talking to me; she crossed the center line. I heard everything as it happened. It's taken me years to get back on track. I know she'd want me to be happy. You make me happy. I'm sorry I behaved the way I did. It was inexcusable."

"We were having a good time. What got into you?"

"I was jealous. I thought you were interested in Cyrus. Then the two drinks came from strangers who were checking you out. All of it set me off. Then, I wasn't sure why. But it didn't take me long to figure it out. You're beyond impressive, Jennifer. I've never seen anyone so quick and so bright as you were when you convinced Cyrus to take the deal to his father. Watching you in action was a turn on. And I'd be lying if I said I didn't find you attractive. I think you're beautiful."

I overlooked the statement. "Did you make the deal?"

"I did. But only because of the way you designed it for me. Of course, Cyrus had to bring something substantial to his father, who was thrilled that his son finally showed a trace of interest in the company. You nailed it. I had no idea you had that in you. I saw your resume, but you're years beyond it. I apologize for everything. I want to see you again."

"We've never seen each other."

"Jennifer, you know what I mean. Don't behave as if you don't."

It was overwhelming. It was obvious he was telling me the truth about how he felt. I could feel it from where I stood. He closed the distance between us. I looked for a cab.

What would happen if I let him in again? The thought was paralyzing. I wasn't in his league. Other than a physical attraction and a mutual interest in business, what more did we have between us? We barely even knew each other. If I went back to that emotional place with him, if I dropped my guard now, he could ruin me later. I had been fortunate before to get out of the situation as quickly as I did. I'd only spent one day with him, and look what that did to me. If I spent more time with him and he pulled anything like that again, he would destroy me. I was that taken by him.

Lisa entered my head. It was from one of our many midnight conversations. *Yes, he could hurt you, Jennifer. But that's true of anyone. At some point, you're going to have to take a risk. Otherwise, you'll be alone forever.*

I felt more conflicted now than I had in my entire life. But some things don't change, so my guard nevertheless went up, with barbed wire along the periphery.

"Alex, I'm happy right now. Your world is complicated. Here, I can make a mark for myself. I'm a manager at one of the city's great restaurants, which beats being someone's arm candy. Right now, I feel as if I'm making a way for myself that's good. I can see myself growing here, and someday elsewhere. I can use this job to get a better job."

"They're lucky to have you. Anyone is lucky to have you."

"I'm lucky to have them. There's no drama here. No jealousy. I can succeed on my own merits. They're offering me that, and I'm grateful for it. I've waited almost five months for it."

Again, I looked for a cab, but I didn't see any, which was ridiculous, especially because the Algonquin Hotel was to my right and the Iroquois was to my left. There should be cabs here. I wanted out. Lisa was waiting up for me, just as she always did to make sure I got home safe. I needed to leave.

He held out his hand to me. I looked down at it. His palm was facing up.

"Alex," I said.

"Just take it, Jennifer. Take it and tell me you don't feel something."

"I have to go."

"Just take my hand. If you feel nothing, I promise I'll disappear and I won't bother you again. But if you feel something, then you'll have the answers to your own questions, because I think you've also been thinking about me."

"How can I not think about you when you call every hour?"

He smiled. "I've been persistent for a reason. Just take my hand. If you feel nothing, I'm gone."

I looked at his hand for a moment. My heart slammed against my chest because I remembered what his touch did to me. I remembered the heat that passed through us the first time he took my hand that night before we entered the elevator. And the second time in the limousine. And all the other times that night before everything changed. Would the feeling be the same? Maybe I did need to know. Maybe this would end it. I reached out and put my hand in his. I looked up at his face and saw how tense he was. He looked worried and vulnerable. His hand closed over mine and he pulled me gently toward him.

"Do you feel it?" he asked.

My eyes filled with tears. Of course, I felt it. But what would that mean for me now? I'd done so well these past several days. As hard as it sometimes was, I'd been focused and determined to walk away from this. Now, here I was again—on the hook and emotionally naked. He squeezed my hand harder and drew me closer to him.

"You're so beautiful," he said.

"I don't know what you see in me."

"More than you see in yourself."

His lips pressed against mine and they were soft, inviting, better than I had imagined. I felt his stubble brush against my chin, and it sent shivers through me. I melted into his kiss because I couldn't deny that I wanted it. He kissed me with a passion and an intensity that surprised me, and I returned it. For a moment, I couldn't get enough of him. It was mutual. He wrapped his arms around my waist tightly enough that I could feel his excitement against my thigh. His tongue swept into my mouth, and I tasted it. He cupped my face with his hands, and kissed my lips, my nose, my forehead, and then the tears that were streaming down my cheeks.

"Why are you crying?"

"I don't know."

"And you're trembling."

I said nothing.

"Tell me."

I turned away from him and wiped my face with the back of my hand. "I don't want to get hurt. I think you might end up hurting me."

"Physically?"

"I don't know. Maybe. You did before. At the very least, I think you will emotionally. I'm so not in your league, Alex. Why don't you find someone who is?"

"Because I want you."

"You don't even know me."

"By sending Blackwell away and by ignoring me over the past week and a half, you've said everything you needed to say about who you are. You're not interested in my money—you gave me back the jewels and the clothes even though you knew they were yours. You could have made a fortune off them, but you didn't. You found a job and moved on. Most wouldn't have done that, because most have an agenda when it comes to me. I have to deal with that every day. I know where you stand with me. I'm grateful for it. Please, let me drive you home."

"I should get a cab."

"There are none."

"One will come."

"Jennifer. It's just a drive home."

But it wasn't. When I got into the back of the limousine with him, his lips were on mine again. He pulled me close and kissed me in ways that no schoolboy had ever kissed me. Once again, I was lost in his embrace.

And I was scared to death of it.

CHAPTER TWENTY-SIX

"Are you hungry?" he asked.

I was nestled in his arms—my head against his chest as I listened to his heartbeat in slow, steady rhythms. He was content. We had been driving around the city for fifteen minutes, and that was the first time he'd said anything to me. We weren't silent—we were saying plenty to each other just by being with each other. Right then, we didn't need words to communicate. It was all laid bare in the thrum of the city.

"I could eat something."

"What would you like?"

"It doesn't really matter."

"You know what I'd love to have?"

"What's that?"

"A burger and fries."

I looked up at him. "You eat junk food?"

"I'm not talking fast food. I'm talking a real hamburger and fries. The good stuff. Fresh."

I poked him in the gut, but there was no gut to be found. There was only the rippling of corded muscles, which nearly sent me over the edge. "Given how in shape you are, I'm assuming it's been five years or so since you've had a burger?"

"Not true."

"When, then?"

"Four nights ago. And it was rare, thick, and juicy. I've got just the place if you want to go."

"What about your waistline?"

"Since when are you concerned about my waistline?"

"Since you obviously are."

"I'll run it off in the morning. You game?"

"I could eat a burger," I said. "But it'll probably go straight to my ass."

He grinned at me. "Good. I like your ass. Let's eat."

* * *

He took me to a restaurant in the East Village. It was nothing more than a hole in the wall, but when

•

we stepped inside, I immediately liked it and its vibe. It was youthful and hip, busy and dim. And it smelled wonderful. It reminded me of some of my favorite diners back home.

"This is great," I said.

"Wait until you have their food."

"How often do you come here?"

"Once a week or so. When I don't want to cook or if I want to disappear during dinner, this is where I go. Nobody would know me or recognize me here."

Rows of red vinyl booths lined the right side of the space. A bar filled with people was to our left. Two booths were free. We chose one, and sat down opposite each other. Although I was wildly over dressed for this place, it didn't matter. There was zero pretension here. It had a neighborhood feel to it. Looking around, it seemed as if everyone knew one another, but not in ways that made you feel like an outsider. It was the perfect choice—casual and happy, but still allowing for pockets of intimacy.

He handed me a menu. "Indulge," he said.

"Where's the good stuff?"

"On the back."

"What are you having?"

"Third burger down. It's topped with blue cheese, red onion, a big slice of a tomato, and some kind of peppery sauce that I want to bottle and bring home. I don't know what it is, but it's great. Obviously, I'm having their hand-cut fries. Maybe a beer."

I put down the menu. "All of that works for me."

"How do you want yours done?"

"They just need to walk the cow past the oven and I'm good."

He laughed at that. It was good to see him laugh. A waiter came by with two glasses of water, and Alex ordered for us. The beers appeared within moments in tall, chilled glasses, and then we were alone.

He lifted his beer toward me. "To a fresh start?"

I took a breath to still my nerves, but then I touched the rim of my glass against his. He'd never know the enormity of the risk I was taking. He'd never understand why it was so difficult for me to trust men. But I had to start. He was sincere earlier. It was clear. It also was time to give him the second chance he wanted. And which I also wanted. There was something between us that was tangible. I couldn't ignore it.

But he won't get a another chance.

"To a fresh start," I said.

We sipped our beers and then he took my hand. "I'm glad you're here."

At that moment, I thought of Lisa. She would be waiting up for me. "Do you mind if I send a text to my roommate? She always stays up for me to make sure I get home safe."

"Of course. It sounds like you have a true friend there."

"Since fifth grade. Lisa's my rock."

I pulled my cell out of my pocket and sent her a text.

"Don't wait up. I'm with Alex. I know. Close your mouth. Get ready for the stories because they're coming. XO."

By the time our food came, we were deep in conversation. Alex asked me everything about my job, and I could tell he wasn't just going through the motions. He asked a dozen questions, the last of which made me smile: "How do I shoe in on that free dinner thing you've got going on?"

"You'll be competing with Lisa, but I'll see what I can do."

"Do you think she'd mind?"

"Lisa loves her food, so it's anyone's guess."

"What does she do?"

"She writes about zombies."

"She writes about what?"

"Zombies. The undead. She's a novelist and she's all about post-apocalyptic worlds and post-mortem flesh. She's very good. Her first and only book so far, was a best seller. She is finishing her new book now. I'm going to proof it soon. I'm beyond proud of her."

"I don't think I could read about zombies."

"She gives them a heart, even if it doesn't beat."

He smiled at me, and I could feel myself slipping away. "Well, whatever you can do about the free dinner thing...."

"I think I can fit you in."

Later, when we were eating one of the best burgers I'd had in a while, I asked him about his own work, and if he was able to move forward the way he wanted to.

"Did Blackwell find someone else for you?"

"No one replaces you," he said. "So I haven't done so, and I won't be doing so. But I'm managing. At least Immaculata isn't talking to me anymore. That's a bonus."

"I told Blackwell that she should hire her for you."

"I know you did, but that isn't happening."

"She was scary."

"There's a reason I hired you. I just didn't know what I was walking into. I'm sorry I behaved the way I did, Jennifer."

I deflected his apology. "How's your burger?"

"Perfect. Yours?"

"I think the cow just touched the stove, so it's perfect. How about your fries?"

"Excellent. Though for some reason—probably because the chef got a look at you—you got more than I did."

"It's all about portion control," I said, pushing my dish toward him. "But here. I can't eat all of this. Dip into my French fry heaven and eat yourself into oblivion." I immediately blushed. "That sounded dirty."

He winked at me. "I know it did."

"But that's not what I meant."

"Something subliminal came over you."

"No, it didn't."

"If a bookstore was open right now, I'd buy you something by Freud and encourage you to question what that really meant."

"I've read Freud."

He snatched one of my fries and popped it into his mouth. "Then you know what I'm talking about."

* * *

When he took me home, I saw him look up at my building, and then I saw the concern on his face when he turned back to me.

"Are you safe here?"

"I'm safe. And we won't be here much longer. We're already looking for a new space. This is what we could afford when we got here."

"Where's your apartment?"

"Fourth floor."

"That's got to be hot."

"We just bought an air conditioner, so it's fine now. Before that, my hair had been a hot mess for most of the summer, so you're right. It's been steamy in all the wrong ways. But we Mainers are tough. Even when it comes to that, uh, particular building."

"Jennifer—"

"It's fine. Lisa and I each have each other's backs, and we're not stupid. We look out for each other. We are nothing if not protective of each other."

"How soon before you move?"

"As soon as we find the right space."

"Let me know if I can help."

"I'll do that." I put my hand on his knee. "I guess this is it."

"For tonight."

"For tonight."

"Thank you for listening to me."

I leaned forward and kissed him full on the mouth. His arms wrapped around me and he pulled me in tight. Somehow, somewhere during the night, with all of its trappings, we got to this point. How did that happen so quickly? How did we get here? Is this how a relationship starts? With a rush? With this intense need to not part? I'd never been involved in anything like this, so I didn't know. He kissed me harder, and I knew even less.

His voice was low when he said, "I wish you were coming home with me."

"That would be a little fast."

"Still."

"Still," I repeated. "This girl is careful. You've probably seen that."

"I probably have."

"Thank you for coming tonight, Alex. I'd written you off. This wasn't easy for me. But I'm glad it happened."

"All I wanted was for you to hear me out. What happened before will never happen again."

Would it? I wasn't sure. But right now this felt good, and I needed to savor it instead of questioning it, which is what I always did with men.

"The burger was beyond," I said. "I hope you liked my French fries."

"You're unbelievable."

"Do you look for innuendoes in everything?"

"When they're that obvious? Yes, I do."

"You seriously need to get some sleep," I said, kissing him again. And again. And maybe once again. "I'll see you soon."

"How soon?"

"I'll let you be the judge of that." With a final kiss that tore through me because he intentionally pressed his tongue against mine, I stepped out of the limo, hurried across the street, pushed my key into the lock, and stepped inside the building, where I knew Lisa would be up and lying in wait.

What the hell was she going to say to me now?

CHAPTER TWENTY-SEVEN

When I walked into the apartment, Lisa was there. Her faithful Kindle was in her hands, and a cold martini made with the good vodka we now could afford was on the table next to her. She lowered her Kindle onto her lap as I moved into the kitchen. I pulled my cell out of my pocket and put it on the counter. Then I saw that she was looking straight at me. Just as I knew she would be.

"Well, well," she said.

"You were right."

"Do tell."

I sat on the sofa and told her about the entire night. I told her about meeting him unexpectedly at db Bistro, about him pouring out his heart to me, about his wife's death, about our late dinner, and all the kissing that happened in between.

"You're in deep now, girl."

"I know I am."

"But I warned you this was coming."

"You were in my head all night."

"I also told you that, at some point in your life, you needed to put your trust in someone, even if they had hurt you once. It happens. But sometimes—if your gut tells you it's the right thing to do—you need to forgive because relationships, sometimes even in their infancy, are difficult. How was he tonight?"

"He kept apologizing. Finally, I needed to stop him. It was genuine. You and I can smell bullshit a farm away."

"Nicely said. I might use that."

"Please do. It's the least I can do."

She sipped her martini.

"Not every man is your father, Jennifer."

"Intellectually, I know that. Emotionally, I've got a lot of work to do when it comes to accepting that."

"When will you see him again?"

"I left that up to him."

"So, it will be tomorrow, then?"

"It's my day off. Anything could happen. Do you think I made the right decision?"

"I know you. You wouldn't have done this if you didn't think it was the right choice. He must be something special if he can break through your walls."

"If this progresses, I'm going to have to tell him at some point."

"About what?"

"You know what."

"That's not going to be easy for you."

"It's not."

"When and if the time is right, you'll know."

"And then there's that other elephant in the room."

"Oh, yeah. That. That's probably going to come up sooner rather than later if this is going where I think it is."

"I'm going to look like an idiot."

"Really? Because he's not going to think that way at all. He's going to look at you like you're his new student."

In the kitchen, my cell buzzed.

"Prince Charming," Lisa said. "I'm assuming you're going to answer this time?"

"That was a text. Hold on."

I went over and read it aloud.

"If you're free at all this week, would you consider being my date one night? I have events I need to go to all week. Otherwise, it will be difficult to get away and see you. Let me know, OK? Maybe tomorrow night? I think you'd especially enjoy tomorrow night. And I don't think I can wait until mid-week. Tonight was wonderful. —Alex."

"A date," Lisa said. "That sounds nice."

"Not that I have anything to wear. I can't afford the sort of dress I'd need to wear at one of those events. There's nothing I can do about that."

"So, tell him the truth. You can't afford it, but you're off tomorrow night, so you can meet him afterwards for a drink somewhere."

"That's not bad."

"Shoot him a text."

I started texting, and when I finished, I read it to Lisa.

"Alex, I need to partially decline—I can't afford a dress, shoes, and everything else for any sort of event. At least not yet, though hopefully soon. But I'd love to meet you for a cocktail afterward. Let me know. I also enjoyed tonight. — Jennifer."

"Not bad," Lisa said.

"I'm about to hit 'send.' Anything else?"

"He's waiting by his phone. Let's see what he says."

I sent the message, and went to the freezer for ice to make my own martini. I needed one. I grabbed a glass from the cupboard, made the drink, shook it with some ice, and poured it straight up to the rim. No olives. I wanted the extra space for the vodka. "Whoever came up with the martini is in the arms of heaven."

"And likely being cradled."

As I sipped, my cell buzzed.

"This will be interesting," Lisa said.

I read the message to myself before reading it aloud to her.

> "I understand. If you'd like, I can have Blackwell pick you up at 10 a.m. This will be fun. I hope you say yes. I already miss you. XO—Alex."

"He's throwing out a lifeline," Lisa said.

"I can't have him buying things for me. I'm not in his employ. This is verging on a relationship. He needs to take me as I am, or not take me at all."

"Are you serious?" she asked.

"I am."

"Oh, please," she said. "Look. Jennifer. Sweetie. Just listen to me for a moment, OK? Grab my laptop for me. I want to show you something I came upon earlier."

I gave it to her.

She opened it, did some typing, and said, "Come here. You need to see this."

I went around her and looked over her shoulder. What I saw was a photograph of Alex. I couldn't read much at this distance because the text was so small, but I did see that the site was *Forbes*.

"I did some research a few days ago. You know, just to see who this guy was. I Googled him. This came up first. I clicked on the article. I got the full picture. I assume after seeing the headline, you also do."

"I can't read all of the text. It's too small from here."

"He's worth about three billion dollars. To be precise, just a shade under. That's the legacy he inherited when his parents died. But props to him because it says here that since their deaths when he took control of Wenn, he's managed to lift his net worth by a half billion. I wouldn't worry about him having Blackwell buy you a dress. Or a pretty necklace. It seriously means nothing to him."

"It doesn't matter," I said. "I feel uncomfortable having him do that for me. We can meet for drinks later. That should be fine."

"Really? And how long do you think that will last? Because I have to tell you, Jennifer, that if, at some point, you really do become serious about this guy, you're going to have to let some of your stubborn Maine pride go. He's high profile. That's what you're getting into. If you become his girlfriend, which is about to happen as far as I'm concerned, this is a natural extension of what that role means. If you're not comfortable with that, cut loose now, because there will be more 'dates' like this in the future. And I really think he means dating in the traditional sense. He wants to be with you. Hell, he's trying to find every way he can to be with you. If you want to explore a relationship with him, then you're going to need to meet him halfway."

I took a breath and looked down at my cell. *I already miss you* was on the screen. *And I already miss you*, I thought. I looked at Lisa. "You know this isn't easy for people like us."

"I get it. But I also know that you're going to have to bend a bit."

"All right." I typed out a text. "Here's what I wrote.

> 'Sounds good. I'll see her at ten. And I can't wait to see you. — Jennifer'"

"That sounds perfect."

"When we meet tomorrow night—"

"You sure as hell don't say, 'I'll return everything tomorrow.' You say, 'Thank you for the dress, Alex. I love it.' And then you plant a kiss on his lips. You make him feel happy and you get on with the night. And, please, enjoy the night. Have fun with him. You work the rest of the week, so you might not be able to see each other again until you have a day off. Make the most of tomorrow."

My cell buzzed. I looked down at his text.

"I know that wasn't easy for you, Jennifer, but I'm happy that you agreed. Just remember that you're taking me out to dinner soon and I have a big appetite. So we're even. See you at eight. Blackwell will fill you in on everything tomorrow. XO—Alex."

When I read it to Lisa, she held up her hand. "Wait a minute. He's going to take some of my food time?"

"We all need to bend a bit...."

"I'm only joking. And I actually love what he just wrote. He gets it. And he's being sensitive about the situation. You can't ask for better than that. You are giving to him what you can, and he's giving to you what he can. It truly is equal." She reached for her martini and held it up toward me. "Cheers, Jennifer. Now, go and get your beauty sleep. The darkness that is Blackwell arrives at ten."

CHAPTER TWENTY-EIGHT

And Blackwell did arrive at ten. Exactly at ten. The buzzer rang, Lisa gave me a peck on the cheek, and out the door I went, wondering exactly how this would go down after our last meeting.

Walking into the stairwell was like walking into a wall of moisture after being in the coolness of the apartment. But I had anticipated the heat and the humidity, and had worn my hair in a simple, chic ponytail that hung down my back. I wore a pair of white Melissa Pants by Akris, and a light-blue sleeveless silk degradé blouse also by Akris. I scored them all at Century 21 during my buying spree after I landed the job at db Bistro, and I got them at a fraction of what I would have paid elsewhere. A pair of nude Jimmy Choo Crown Peep-Toe platform pumps, also purchased during the spree, completed the look.

When I opened the door, Blackwell was standing just beyond it in a light, elegant suit perfect for the day's weather. She immediately assessed what I was wearing. "Very pretty, Jennifer. Love the shoes, love the hair, love the pants."

"What about the blouse?" I asked with a smile.

"Love it."

"Thank you."

"I'm happy to see you again."

"I'm sorry I was difficult last time."

"There's no need to apologize. Alex and I have talked over the past week, and I think I have a clearer idea of what happened that night. I'm glad you gave him a second chance. That probably wasn't easy to do given what happened."

I wasn't going to share anything personal with her, so I didn't engage her.

She motioned to the limousine behind her. "Shall we? I skipped the donuts this time, but I did buy us each a coffee at Starbucks. They might have a bit of espresso in them. OK, they probably have a lot."

"I have a feeling we're going to need it."

"My thoughts exactly."

We started to walk to the car. The driver got out, and held open the rear door for us.

"Alex said that you'd fill me in on where we're going tonight."

"Big event at the Museum of Natural History. And it's a fun event, which is why he wanted you to come. Have you ever been there before?"

"I haven't."

"You'll love it. Dramatic doesn't even begin to explain what you'll see tonight. The lighting alone. God! Not to mention the whale in Milstein Hall, which is where you'll have dinner with about five hundred other lucky people. The food is always very good there. And the cocktails define decadence."

We slipped inside the car, the driver closed the door, and we were off.

"What's the event for?"

Blackwell handed me my coffee. "It's their annual fundraising gala. Be prepared for the people you'll see. It won't just be society, though they'll be lurking around with their tight faces. What makes it such a fun night is that it's a big draw for celebrities. You'll see everyone who's in town tonight, and a few who will fly in for the occasion. It's black tie, but it's a looser mix. Everyone knows everyone."

"Except me."

"Doesn't matter. By the end of the night, everyone will know who you are. Shall we try Bergdorf again? Good. Then Van Cleef? I'm thinking vintage. I'm thinking twenties. I'm thinking *Gatsby*. Then we give ourselves over to Bernie. I bribed him again, but it was easier this time. He loved working with you before. He thinks you're a natural beauty, and Bernie doesn't compliment just anyone. Believe me. We'll get ready at Wenn, just like last time. Then you can meet Alex on his floor. Sound good?"

Sounds overwhelming.

"Sounds perfect," I said.

"Then let's do this. You've got one romantic night ahead of you."

"Won't Alex be working tonight?"

She sipped her coffee and looked at me over the rim. "Not tonight. He made that very clear to me. Tonight, it's all about spending time with you."

* * *

At Bergdorf, Blackwell went on a bender, and she wasn't messing around. When we arrived, a striking woman around Blackwell's age met us at the door with an extendend hand, which I shook.

"I'm Pauline Barreau," she said. "It's good to meet you, Ms. Kent. I've heard much about you."

What has she heard?

"Ms. Blackwell and I spoke late last night, and we had a meeting of the minds. If you'll follow me, I'll take you to a private dressing area to show you the dress we both think will be perfect for you tonight. It's something that will set you apart from the rest."

Late last night? I got home around one. I agreed to go to the event with Alex around one-thirty. He must have got Blackwell on the phone and told her to make this happen.

At that moment, I felt for her. But when I turned to look at her, it was clear that she was in her element and was getting off on this. She once told me that she loved fashion, so maybe this was fun for her. Maybe she saw it as a day off. I hoped so.

We went to a dressing room on the third floor, and I got a sense by how private it was that only a select few were allowed back here.

"Champagne?" Pauline asked.

"No, thank you," I said.

"Ms. Blackwell?"

"Tempting as it is, Pauline, I also must pass. Jennifer and I are mainlining caffeine this morning. Why don't we see the dress? You know I'm dying to see it in person. You're so cruel, Pauline, making me wait like this."

Pauline arched an eyebrow in amusement. "Cruel, Ms. Blackwell?"

"Evil."

"Give me a moment."

"I've waited hours for this moment."

"Just a moment more...."

"God!"

She left through a mirrored door and returned with a sheer blue dress that seemed to float through the air as she carried it toward us. It looked weightless to me until she held it up, allowing it to drop, and Blackwell and I were able to see the front of the dress, which was laden with an intricate pattern of crystals.

"Swarovski Elements," Blackwell said, circling the garment without touching it. "The design of the crystals is divoon, Pauline. Beyond divoon. Divoon to the tenth power. Very twenties. Very now. So on trend. Miu Miu designed the dress, Jennifer. Isn't it fantastic?" She was so caught up in the moment, she just charged forward, not allowing me to speak. I kind of loved her when she was like this. She became more human to me. "The blue is just right. Soft. Muted. Slate undertones." She pointed a finger at Pauline. "Just as you said there'd be." Then, she looked at me. "The color will work with your hair and with your skin. I think we've found it. I think this is it." She put her hand to her chest. "Two in a row!"

"Perhaps Ms. Kent should try it on before we get too excited."

"Right, right," Blackwell said, composing herself. "Jennifer, follow Pauline and try on the dress. I'm too stressed out to think that it won't fit. We know the obstacles—your tantrum of a derriere being the real challenge. Naturally, I'm concerned. Pauline, you have a tailor for me, don't you?"

"I do."

"And this can happen today if it doesn't fit?"

"I can make it happen within an hour."

"*Je t'aime.*"

I went into a large changing room surrounded by mirrors, and put on the dress. I then looked at myself, and just stopped for a moment. Was this really my life? I'd been here once before, but again? Really? The dress was stunning. I could only imagine what

I'd look like when Bernie was finished with me. I turned this way and that way, and I heard my father's voice in my head.

Don't think you're all that, girl.

"I don't," I said to him in the mirrors. "But I'm working on it. You won't hold me back forever. And you won't be in my head for the rest of my life, either. I'm getting rid of you, you son of a bitch. I'm moving forward."

I took a breath and walked out of the changing room, knowing I was about to be judged by Blackwell in the dressing room, which intimidated me. In some ways, her criticism reminded me of my father, and so I braced myself for whatever she had to say.

But there was no judgment. When she saw me, she held up her hands in what looked to me like a show of relief. She turned to Pauline in what looked to me like a show of gratitude, and then she told me to turn, turn, turn so she could see, see, see. When I finished, laughing, she said, "Can you believe this? We just need a nip and a tuck above her ass, and we're good! God!"

* * *

Later, after leaving Bergdorf, we went to Van Cleef & Arpels on Fifth, and Blackwell, who apparently already had spoken to one of the managers, introduced me to him.

"This is Christopher," she said. "Christopher, Jennifer Kent. Are we good? Great, because time is running out. Did you find anything that comes close to what I had in mind?" she asked him.

"I did. I've chosen a few statement pieces. Vintage pieces from the twenties."

"You're too good. So smart. Let's see."

In a private room at the back of the store, he showed us a bracelet that made me catch my breath. It was a line bracelet, streamlined in design, with geometric panels indicative of the Art Deco period. The diamonds and sapphires that encompassed it were set in platinum.

"Try it on," Blackwell said.

I held out my wrist, and Christopher fastened the bracelet around it. Before I could admire it, Blackwell took hold of my wrist and turned it over. Her eyes flicked up to Christopher's.

"You'll need to take out two links," she said. "Otherwise, it's fantastic. Jennifer? Thoughts?"

"It's beautiful."

She turned back to Christopher. "You have matching earrings?"

He did. I tried them on. They were large sapphire teardrops framed with tiny, delicate diamonds also set in platinum. Blackwell held my chin in her hand, appraised them, approved of them, and bought them. In a cloud of disbelief, I watched her shower Christopher with a flourish of air kisses before I followed her out of the building and onto the sidewalk. She led me to the limousine waiting for us curbside, and we stepped inside.

"Success," she said.

"I don't know how you do it."

"I love fashion. Absolutely live for it. So far, today has been like a vacation for me. Thank you."

I didn't know what to say. Being treated like this was humbling.

"You're probably hungry," she said. "So am I, even if the very idea of eating repels me. No one should eat—ever. But I suppose we have to don't we? Of course, we do. Otherwise, we'll just end up looking like shit in a coffin, which absolutely will not do, unless we're cremated. There's a thought. No one will know then. Hmmmm. But I'm getting ahead of myself. Salad? Something light? We've got time."

"Sure," I said.

"I suggest a salad for you. Some hardcore roughage. Give it an hour or two, and it will clear you out. You'll thank me later."

"Isn't that was the Spanx is for?"

"Spanx can only do so much, Jennifer. Trust me. We're talking total body cleanse here. Let's do it. Let's get rid of whatever's in you."

I looked at her and blushed.

* * *

It was just after four o'clock when we arrived at a very simple and understated salad bar on Park called, "Salade."

"It looks cheap because it is cheap. It's a damned hole in the wall, but it's clean, well managed, and painstakingly attended to. It's über fresh and, in a weird kind of way, it's kind of fabulous. You don't always have to spend the kind of money we just spent to get the results you want. I come here almost every day. Salad, salad, salad. Thin, thin, thin. Slim, slim, slim. Nothing, nothing, nothing. Eat what I tell you to eat, and you'll send me roses me tomorrow."

"Is that your favorite flower?"

"God, no."

"What is?"

"Why do you want to know?"

"I'm just curious."

"You're going to judge me for this."

"No, I won't."

"Yes, you will, but it is what it is. The flower is very rare. You can hardly find it, and if you do, it's in the low-lying tropical rainforests of Indonesia. It's the Corpse Flower."

Of course, it is.

"Don't you dare make a face at me, Jennifer. It's endangered--but who or what isn't? My wardrobe is endangered at the end of every season. It just dies in my closets, and then I have the lot of it thrown out. God! The flower smells like crap, it dies within a week, and yes, it eats flies and other bugs to survive, but when it's bloom, it's divoon. It's almost a meter wide. And it's gorgeous. I love it."

"Who knew?" I said.

When we went to the salad bar, which was enormous, Blackwell was precise in what she wanted me to eat. "Take the romaine. Get the spinach. No, no—more of it. And the arugula. Don't be so prissy, Jennifer. Jesus. Pile it on. We came here for a cleanse. Now, the endive. That's right. And the bib lettuce. And the radicchio. Look at you. Perfect. Try the frisée. Not that. That's iceberg. God! It's the other one. That's right. The one that looks like it's been electrocuted. Get lots of that. Oh, and the watercress and the mache. Yes, that's right, those. Finish it all with a *small* drop of oil and a huge dollop of fresh lemon and vinegar, and you're on your way to an A. What are you doing? Don't you dare touch the salt!"

"What about tomatoes?" I said. "Mushrooms? Cucumbers and peppers? Maybe one of those hard-boiled eggs right there. I'd love to have one of those."

"Are you serious? Those will only add bulk. You've got a pound of greens there—you're fine as you are. You should be happy I'm letting you eat, period. Just enjoy what you have and lie in wait. The effects will hit by the time we get back to Wenn. You'll see. I don't want to be anywhere near you when it happens, but it'll happen. Just tell me when you need to use the restroom, I'll point you in the general direction, and then I'll seal myself in my office. You'll lose a good pound."

"But Alex likes my ass," I said to her with a smile.

She rolled her eyes at me. "Oh, Maine. You'll never lose it there. Obviously. Let's eat."

* * *

Later that night, the shopping and salads behind us, I indeed felt a gastrointestinal rumbling and ran to the restroom. How did Blackwell know these secrets? When it was all said and done, my abs felt flatter than they had in months. Bonus!

When I returned to her office, she swept me with a glance. "See?' she said. "Look at you. Flat."

"How do you know all this?"

"I just do."

"But how?"

"When Alex's mother was alive, we were great friends, which is probably why Alex views me as family. I always was around, fussing over him because I knew that Constance was distracted. Anyway, we did everything together, including every fad diet going. The one thing that always worked for us was the greens. We'd do a cleanse once a month, and drop five pounds. It just works."

"What was his mother like?"

"That's a loaded question."

"Why?"

"Because Constance was Constance. She was difficult. Naturally, I loved her for it. We mixed perfectly. Many also consider me difficult—though I have *no* idea why—so it's no wonder we were fast friends. To others, she was a complete snob. Even Alex thought so. He loved his mother, but he didn't like her very much. He had issues with her. Still does, I think. But to me, she was just a perfectionist. What Alex never understood is that she was in the public eye and had a lot to live up to. Because of the position she assumed in this city, she underwent massive scrutiny. There was no room for error or failure. In the beginning, the press was relentless with her. Truly awful, especially because she was so young when her husband became so successful. She didn't have anyone to lean on or to show her how to do things properly. As a result, she made mistakes. It was tough on her, but she learned from them. Did she become bitter because of the criticism? Probably. Who wouldn't? Did she pass that bitterness down to Alex? I think so. They never were close. Constance always was thinking about her next party, not about what was best for Alex. Sometimes, I think he was their only child for a reason. Constance didn't want more children. She had too much to manage as it was and as far as she was concerned, he was it."

"That must have been difficult for Alex. He must have sensed it."

"Of course he did."

"In my own way, I know how that feels."

"But you're here, aren't you? You made the decision to leave Maine and come to Manhattan for a reason. Your past is your past, and what I sense in you, Jennifer, is that yours was an unpleasant past. Remember this. Whatever happened to you then should remain in your past, but it also should inform your present and your future. Never forget that."

"I would think that having a mother like Alex's would make someone mistrust women."

"Initially, I think that was true for Alex. He didn't date much in high school or college. I don't remember any girlfriends. But when he met Diana, everything changed. They had a wonderful marriage. I was happy for him because I could see how happy *he* was. And then, just like that, she was gone. He told you about her death, didn't he?"

"He did."

"He's been single ever since. Losing her crushed him. It's been four years, and I know for a fact, that since then, he has seen no one. It's been all about work for him. He's here seven days a week. Always works late. I think he's been running from Diana's death since it happened. And then you walked into his life. You may have begun with a business arrangement with him, but he never saw you coming. He told me what happened that night. What he did was immature and idiotic—I told him so. I chastised him. Then he told me that he was unprepared for you. He said you found Cyrus good looking. Alex is only human. He got jealous and frankly, he acted like an asshole."

"Why are you telling me all this?"

"Because you keep asking questions."

"But you don't need to answer them."

She leaned back in her chair. "I want to see him happy again. I want that spark to come back in his eyes. And it's starting to return because of you. Earlier, when I thanked you for giving him a second chance, I meant it. Not just anyone would have given back those jewels, Jennifer. You know they were yours to keep. You know you could have sold them. Giving them back to him told me everything I needed to know about you. I'm quietly encouraging this. Whether it works out or not is between you two."

She looked at her watch. "You should get changed. Bernie will be here in ten minutes, and he's never late. How do you want to wear your hair tonight?"

"I want to wear it down."

"With that dress? Why?"

"Because that's how Alex likes it," I said.

* * *

An hour later, when Bernie stepped away from me and glanced at Blackwell, I noticed that she returned her approval with a smile.

"Can I see?" I asked.

"There's the mirror," Blackwell said. "Have a look."

I stood in front of it and couldn't still a rush. The dress was slimming and stunning. Even in this dim light, the crystals were alive and glinting from my breasts to the bottom of the dress in intricate patterns that evoked the twenties. Bernie had flat ironed my hair, and it moved along with the dress, the material of which was so delicate, it wafted in the air when I turned.

"How do you feel?" Blackwell asked.

"Like I'm looking at someone else. The earrings and the bracelet are so pretty. Just perfect. I love what you did with my hair, Bernie, and with my makeup. The eye shadow brings out the blue in the dress, as well as the sapphires."

"That was the idea," he said.

"I only regret one thing," Blackwell said. She came around and faced me. "I should have gone with a necklace. With so many crystals, I thought it would be too much. Overkill. But I was wrong." She looked over at Bernie. "Wasn't I?"

"It's not as bad as you think. If her hair was up and off her shoulders, I'd agree. She would have needed something at her throat because the dress is strapless. And with so much skin exposed, it would have looked as if something was missing. But with her hair down? It softens what's lacking. This will do just fine, but, yes, it could have been better with a matching necklace." I saw him look at her. "You know I won't lie to you, my love."

"Which is one of the many reasons you're here." She turned to me. "So, next time a necklace. Or at least a necklace on standby. You still look fabulous, Jennifer. And now you should go. It's nearly eight and he'll be waiting for you."

I felt a pit grow and then unravel in my stomach. Just knowing I was about to see Alex again made me at once nervous and excited. *From burger joints to this. All within twenty-four hours.*

With Blackwell at my side, we walked to the elevator. She pressed one of the buttons, and then she lifted her face to mine. "Remember," she said. "Forget the past. Enjoy tonight."

The elevator door slid open.

"I'll have a martini in your honor."

She looked weirdly irritated with me. "If you must," she said as I stepped into the waiting car. "But at the very least, choose the Skinny Girl vodka, Jennifer. I didn't pack you full of roughage and ask you to go through that mini-cleanse for nothing."

"I don't remember you asking me," I said.

"You know what I mean."

"Thank you, Ms. Blackwell."

"It's Barbara. Now, go have fun."

CHAPTER TWENTY-NINE

When the elevator doors opened, Alex stood beyond them, just as he had the last time, with his hands in his pockets and a grin on his face.

Only this time wasn't like the last time. This time was different. We were moving in a new direction that became immediately apparent when he held out his hand for mine and drew me close to him. He kissed me lightly on the lips. Then, in my ear, in a voice that was so low, it was beyond sexy, he said, "You look beautiful."

"Thank you."

He admired my dress. "That should get some attention."

"It might even blind a few people."

He arched an eyebrow at me. "It would make for an interesting night if it did." He reached out and gently touched my hair. "I love it when you wear your hair down."

"I know you do."

"Did you do it for me?"

"I might have given it a thought."

"I'm glad that you did. Do you remember when we officially met? At the interview? We were talking, you pulled out a pin in your hair, it tumbled down your back, and I was transfixed. Then, it was wavy. Now, it's straight. Either way, I love it. When I think of you, this is how I imagine you. With your hair down. With it falling down your back. With you shaking it out with your hands in an effort to cool yourself, if only for an instant."

I could feel myself starting to get warm. "Here," I said, wanting to take the attention off me. "Let me have a look at you." I pulled away from him, and he put his hands back in his pockets, cocked his head to one side, and grinned. "Very handsome, Mr. Wenn."

"Thank you, Ms. Kent."

"But then I love you in a tux. *And* in a suit."

"Why's that?"

"If we were to psychoanalyze the situation, it likely would come down to some Prince Charming fantasies I had as a kid. You know, someone who would sweep me away from all that I wanted to forget."

"What did you want to forget?"

"I've forgotten," I lied. "And it doesn't matter now, because here he is. Right in front of me."

"You don't say?"

"I do say."

"Why do I want to devour you right now?"

"Probably for the same reasons I want to tackle you. But Bernie worked hard, so we'll respect that."

"We better change the subject or my hands are going to be all over you."

"And that's a bad thing?"

"Jennifer...."

"Blackwell and I had fun today," I said. "I don't know how she does it, but that woman is nothing if not on her game."

"She always has been. My mother loved her for it. I've always thought they should name a hurricane after her."

"It would need to be Category 5. Why shortchange her?"

"Good point." He paused for a moment. "Would you mind turning around for me? Just so I can see the rest of the dress?"

I started to turn, but then he put his hand on my shoulder and stopped me so my back was to him. "I want to have a long look," he said. "Do you mind?"

His hand resting on my bare shoulder was almost enough to do me in. But then he removed it and I heard him take a step back.

"Did you pick this out?"

"Blackwell did."

"Blackwell has an eye." His voice was off to my left. Then, I heard him come up behind me. "In fact, I know she does. With her help, I picked out this."

Over my head came a diamond and sapphire necklace that made me catch my breath when I caught a glimpse of it as he moved my hair aside and fastened it around me. *Blackwell*, I thought. *Missing a necklace, indeed.*

The stones were cool against my neck. "Alex," I said.

"My gift to you."

"But all of this is a gift from you."

"May I see?"

I turned to him with my hand pressed against the stones.

"You'll need to lower your hand, Jennifer."

"Sorry. I don't know what to say."

"I say it's beautiful. What do you think? There's a mirror to your left. Look."

I turned and saw that the necklace was in the same family as the other jewels. A delicate clutch of diamonds circled my neck, followed by a single, vertical line of three larger diamonds at my throat. At the end of that was a large teardrop sapphire surrounded by smaller diamonds that set just above my cleavage.

"It's gorgeous," I said. "I don't know what to say."

"There's no need to say anything."

"Yes, there is." I kissed him, but not as gently as before. I pressed against him with every bit of raw emotion I had within me. I leaned full into his kiss, which probed deep. With his body so close to mine, I could feel all of him against me, some of it pulsing. When we pulled away, the collateral damage was clear—he was practically wearing my lipstick. "Here," I said, opening the clutch Blackwell let me borrow. "Tissues. Let me fix that."

"Before you do, how about this first?" He went in for the kill again. Only this time, his hands smoothed down my sides and rested on my ass, which he squeezed, and then gripped. He pulled me firmly against him so I knew exactly what he was feeling.

My nipples hardened when he did that. A shiver shot through me. I'd never experienced anything like this before, but then I'd never dated anyone before. Still, plenty of other men had tried to catch my eye over the years. Why was this so different? Why did I feel such a strong connection to Alex? Is this what it felt like when you met the 'one'? I had no idea. I wished Lisa were here so I could ask her, because she'd know. She'd been in two long-term relationships. She'd be able to tell me what I was feeling, and why. As for me, this was foreign territory. He'd turned me on so much that I was dizzy with desire. When he kissed me, it felt as if my heart was shaking. A moment later, when he stopped with a gentle bite to my lower lip that obviously was designed to send me to the outer reaches of the universe, where I thought I saw a comet or a nebula, I somehow managed to pull it together and look at him.

"You're going to do me in."

"That's the plan."

"I'm glad you have a plan. Very resourceful of you. And by the way, what was that?"

"What was what?"

"That bite thing you did?"

"Just something I thought you might like. Was I wrong?"

"You weren't wrong."

"You should see what else I can do with my teeth and my tongue."

"Stop."

"No, really. You should see."

"Alex."

"Why are your eyes unfocused?"

"Because I can't handle being manhandled." I lifted my head to the ceiling and collected myself. When I looked at him again, I saw the mischief in his eyes. "Why are you doing this to me?"

"Because you want me to."

I didn't know how to respond to that, so I said, "I need to blot your lips again."

"Please do."

I blotted.

"Am I good to go?" he asked.

"One more swipe."

"I kind of like you on my lips."

"I kind of like *me* on your lips."

"You might want to look in the mirror," he said.

"Oh, no." I looked and saw that my lipstick was gone, but at least it hadn't smeared. After all of Bernie's work, that would have been a disaster. I pulled out the tube of lipstick Blackwell left for me in the clutch and reapplied.

"Are we finished?" I asked.

"For now."

"Then let's get out of here before we decide to stay."

* * *

When we arrived at the museum, the building's facade was lit in bright oranges and deep reds. People were walking up the wide stone steps to the entrance.

Camera flashes popped. The steps were roped off to allow entrance only for the guests, but there were crowds on the sidelines and they were cheering. I remembered what Blackwell said—this was a major draw for celebrities. Given the sheer amount of photographs that were being taken, that appeared to be an understatement.

"Are you nervous?" Alex asked.

"Not at all."

"Get ready for the press."

"They need to get ready for my dress. I'm about to be lit up like a disco ball."

"Who better?" he asked.

* * *

We were twenty minutes inside the Theodore Roosevelt Rotunda—the walls of which also were set ablaze with concealed orange lighting—when I saw a man looking directly at Alex and me.

Given the distraction of the towering and show-stopping brontosaurus skeleton, the crowds—and the famous faces within the crowds—I was surprised that I noticed him at all. But he was looking so openly at us, and with such anger, it was difficult to miss him. He was an older man, somewhere in his late fifties, and he looked familiar to me. I'd seen him before.

Where?

I lifted my martini to my lips and spoke, but didn't sip. "Why is that man staring at us?"

"Which man?"

"Near the skeleton. Gray hair. Fifties. Very tan. He's looked away a few times, but he keeps turning back. He's looking at us now, and he looks pissed. Who is he?"

"Someone who would rather see me dead."

I looked up at him. "That's kind of harsh."

"It's the truth."

"What are you talking about?"

"Let's walk over here."

We joined the milling crowds and stopped beside one of the glowing walls, which Alex leaned against, thus keeping his back to the mystery man and me squarely facing him so we could talk in private.

"His name is Gordon Kobus."

"Kobus Airlines," I said. "Of course. I knew I knew him. His company is about to go under. I've read about it."

Alex shook his head at me. "Jennifer, what don't you know?"

"I told you I'm a business junkie. I live for this stuff. Just don't ever ask me to sew anything for you. Like a button on one of your suits. I'd ruin it, and that would kill me for reasons you already know."

"Noted."

"Kobus just applied for emergency funding from the government."

"It did."

"One of the stories said that the board is also seeking new investors. But they likely won't have time to secure either. Because of the size and the good condition of the fleet, too many are ready to sweep in and take over the company for themselves, hostile or otherwise." And then I just looked at Alex when it came to me. "Which is you, right? Wenn Air. You're planning a takeover. You want to add his fleet to your own."

It wasn't a question it was a statement.

"I do," Alex said. "We're in the early stages now—we're wooing management in an effort to get them on our side, which hasn't exactly been difficult. They're finished with him. He knows it, and you're right—Gordon isn't having any of it." He shrugged. "I don't blame him. Kobus used to be his baby, but he's put baby in the corner for years. He didn't mind the store. He's lived a playboy lifestyle for a decade now, he didn't listen to his board, he didn't listen to counsel, and now it's all caught up with him. I plan on taking his company from him and merging it with my own. We'll give his fleet Wenn's first-class treatment, and manage it successfully."

"How soon?"

He shrugged. "Not sure. Depends on management. But these things take time. If they're for it, we can finish this by winter. If they resist, then we get more aggressive. We apply pressure, and then we make our intentions public. Then it really gets ugly. Either way, we're going forward with it."

I clinked my martini glass against his and we knocked them back.

"That was refreshing," I said.

"The martini or the talk of the takeover?"

"Both."

He looked at me sincerely. "I'm glad you're here, Jennifer. I don't think you know what it means to me. I could talk with you all night. I know it's still early, but I hope you're having a good time."

I certainly was back at Wenn. "I just talked about takeovers with someone who not only understands what they are, but who actually does them. Are you joking? I'm in my element. Oh, and by the way, I look like I'm straight out of *Gatsby* and I have the night's smartest, best-looking date. Because of you, I'm having a fabulous time."

I took his free hand in mine and our fingers interlocked. There were no other words to express how I felt. He tightened his grip, and then he leaned forward to give me a quick peck on the cheek.

"Your stubble is going to do me in."

"You like that?"

"Please, don't tease me."

"You haven't even seen me tease you yet," he said.

* * *

Later, when dinner was announced, we followed the crowd to Milstein Hall, which caused me to pause when we descended the steps that led to the massive space. It was lit in rippling hues of blue that evoked the ocean, and it was filled with fifty tables set for ten. Hovering just below the glass ceiling was an enormous replica of a blue whale that I thought had to be close to a hundred feet long. I'd never seen anything like it. It was magical.

My father entered my head again and started his bullshit rant about how I didn't belong here, but I mentally shook him away. Or at least, I tried to. I looked around at the sea of celebrities, people I had seen for years on television and in movies, or musicians I admired, and I knew he was right. Who was I to be here? It made no logical sense.

But I am here, I thought. And *I'm here for a reason. Where did these people come from? Did all of them come from a privileged life? Or did they work for it? I'm betting most worked for it. I bet, just like me, most never thought they'd see anything like this.*

"Are you OK?" Alex asked.

I realized I was gripping his hand more firmly than before, and I forced myself to relax. "I'm fine. It's just so much. It's beautiful."

At the bottom of the stairs, one of the hosts greeted us and took us to our table, where none other than Immaculata Almendarez herself was seated.

"This should be interesting," I said quietly.

"She planned it," he said. "So, it *will* be interesting. Get ready."

Naturally, when the host seated us, Alex was placed directly beside Immaculata, while I was asked to take the seat between him and an older gentleman.

"Alex," Immaculata said, turning to look at him. "What a surprise."

"Really? I was thinking, 'What a coincidence.'"

"You're so funny." She leaned forward to look at me, and I saw her eyes go to the diamonds and sapphires at my ears, neck and wrist. "And I see you're still with Jane."

"It's Jennifer," I said.

"Right, right. Why do I always think of you as a Jane?"

"I'm not sure, Immaculata. The only thing I can imagine is that as we get older, our capacity to remember things begins to fail."

"It begins to what?"

"Fail. Like our hearing, for instance. You should have yours checked. Our bodies eventually betray us."

"Mine hasn't yet," she said as she pressed her fingertips against the table, and arched her back toward them and it, thus allowing us all to glimpse the full weight of her formidable breasts, which were barely covered by her plunging black dress. I thought she looked desperate, and I didn't mind when she reached for Alex's hand when she turned her attention to him. "How are you?" she asked.

"Working hard, Immaculata."

"You always work so hard."

"Not as much since I've been with Jennifer, but work is work. And work is good." He casually removed his hand from hers and signaled for a waiter. "Wenn keeps me busy. Jennifer keeps me busy in other ways."

Immaculata swallowed that poison pill as if it was a clear glass of water. I had to give it to her—she was cool. "The last time I saw you was two weeks ago. At The Met fundraiser. I saw you both leave in such a hurry. Everyone was buzzing about it."

Oh, she wasn't going to go there.

"There was an undercurrent," she said. "It didn't look good. People said Jennifer removed her jewels and then some overheard a choice exchange of words. It was on everyone's lips for a week. I've been worried about you, especially because I haven't seen you."

She was talking to him as if I wasn't at the table. I rested my chin in the palm of my hand, turned to her, and just listened with a half-smile.

The waiter Alex signaled stopped by the table.

"Would you like a drink, sir?"

"Actually, we'd like another table. I see only half the room is seated at this point, so it shouldn't be an issue. Please tell your host that Alexander Wenn and Jennifer Kent would prefer to be seated elsewhere. Or I can do that for you."

"I'd be happy to assist you, sir."

Conversation at the table stopped. Everyone who was pretending not to listen to Immaculata's conversation with Alex started to listen and watch openly as the moment stretched and unfolded.

"Alex," Immaculata said. "I didn't mean—"

"Yes, you did. You meant everything. And I'm tired of it. I don't play games—ever. You will not insult Jennifer—ever—even if you fail when you try to do so. She's smarter and quicker than you. You should have learned that by now."

"I don't know what you're talking about."

One man at the opposite end of the table cleared his throat.

I felt a sudden rush of affection for Alex. He was finished with her. He pushed back his chair and stood, and then he gently pulled back my chair so I could stand next to him.

"Have a fine evening, Immaculata," Alex said. "And please remember what you learned in boarding school."

"Boarding school?"

"That's right, boarding school."

"What did I learn in boarding school?"

"Obviously not your manners, because they have been absent since we were seated next to you. Good night."

He took my hand and turned to find the host. "Is there another table for us? Or should we leave?"

"Of course there's another table for you, Mr. Wenn. Right this way."

"Thank you," he said.

As we cut through the crowd, he pulled me near him in such a way that was at once protective, possessive, and apologetic. "I'm not going to promise that won't happen again, but if it does with another person, the results will be the same. No one treats you like that in front of me."

He was furious. I could feel his anger coming off him in waves.

"It's OK," I said, wanting to calm him down. "I got in a few licks."

"You did," he said. "But this town can go to hell before that happens again. And I'm sorry that it happened. We never should have sat next to her in the first place. I should have known better. I should have asked for another table when I saw that she'd set us up. I wasn't thinking. I apologize."

I dodged a waiter coming toward us with a lifted tray of cocktails, ducked my head, heard his apology, and kept moving. "There's no need to."

"Yes, there is."

"Then, thank you."

"You're my girlfriend," he said. "There's no need to thank me. No one treats my girlfriend like that. OK?" He turned to look at me, and I could see on his face just how furious he was with the situation. "OK?"

"OK," I said.

He put his hand against my back, and we walked together toward our new table. He'd just called me his girlfriend twice, and this was only our second legitimate date. That is, if we were considering burgers at the diner a date. What the hell was I to make of that?

Nothing.

Because, if I was being honest with myself, what he just said is exactly what I wanted to hear. We'd moved beyond the past and into another stage. I was his girlfriend. And I was as thrilled about it as I was nervous about it.

What the hell was I going to do when he wanted to become intimate?

CHAPTER THIRTY

The next week passed in a blur. And while I didn't see Alex as much as I wanted to because we both worked nights—me at the restaurant, he at the events he needed to attend—we met twice for breakfast, we spoke when we could by phone, we texted each other throughout the day, and he always picked me up when the restaurant closed.

Each night, he was fresh from a party and in a tuxedo, looking dashing. Though increasingly, he also looked either distracted or stressed. Tonight was no exception.

When I left the restaurant, he was leaning against the limousine with his feet crossed at the ankles and his arms folded across his chest. He smiled when he saw me, and we kissed for a long, lingering moment, but something was off. I could sense it, and I had to wonder if he was having second thoughts about reigniting this relationship, probably because we still hadn't slept together. By today's standards, that should have happened after the event at the museum. But, despite his efforts, it didn't.

At the end of the night, he asked me up to his penthouse at Wenn and made an effort to progress in that direction, but I told him I wasn't ready. He said there was no hurry, but he might go nuts if he had to wait much longer. He had no clue that I was still a virgin. And he didn't know the reasons why I was still a virgin. At some point, if I was going to continue this relationship with him, I would have to tell him all that I needed to tell him about me and my past. Sooner rather than later. It was unfair to him otherwise.

When we were in the limousine, I put my hand on his leg, and he wrapped his arm around my shoulder. "Hey," he said.

"How do you feel about taking me to your place tonight?" I asked. "I need to talk to you about something. Well, a few things, actually."

"Is everything all right?"

"I just need to talk to you, Alex."

"That sounds ominous."

He lived on the top two floors of Wenn, where his parents once lived. The space was now his. When I first saw it, I wasn't surprised to find how beautifully designed and decorated it was. Save for the colorful, original paintings on the walls, everything was white, from the furniture to the marble floors. At this height, the city views beyond the sweeping surround of windows were spectacular.

"Would you like something to drink?" he asked when we stepped out of his private elevator and into the foyer.

"A martini would be nice."

"You *are* a martini girl, aren't you?"

"Guilty."

"Actually, after today, I wouldn't mind one myself. Give me a few minutes. If you'd like, take off your shoes and relax in the living room. You've been on your feet all night."

"You sound tense," I said as I moved into the room.

"A little. But we'll save talking about that for another time. Right now, I just want to be with you."

Why is he tense?

I looked out at the views, listened to him shake our drinks in the kitchen, and then turned to him when he entered the living room with them. He handed me mine, and we touched glasses. He kissed me meaningfully on the mouth, and we took a sip before sitting down next to each other on the leather sofa.

"Have I told you that you look beautiful tonight, Jennifer?"

"Maybe once or twice. And I'll repeat—you look very handsome yourself, Mr. Wenn."

"How was work?"

"Busier than usual. You?"

We sat on the sofa.

"Another time. What's on your mind? You've made me curious."

My stomach started to turn, but there was no stopping this now. I had to go through with it. I took a sip of my martini, and put it on the table in front of us. "Alex, I need to tell you something."

He didn't respond. He just stared at me, concern and maybe even a trace of fear on his face. But why fear? Did he think I was going to break this off?

"This is going to sound ridiculous," I said. "I'm twenty-five, for God's sake."

"Jennifer, nothing you have to say to me is going to sound ridiculous."

"Are you sure? Because here's one for you. I've never been with anyone before."

His brow furrowed as if he didn't understand.

Just say it.

"I'm a virgin."

His eyes widened. "You're a virgin?"

I nodded and felt a rush of shame. There were reasons why I had never given myself to a man. Reasons that made me feel insecure in this relationship now.

"Is that why, you know, the other night...?"

"That's right."

A weight seemed to lift off him. And there was something else, something in his eyes. A thrill? He reached for my hand. "You didn't need to tell me that."

"Yes, I did. You needed to know. I can't expect you to wait for me forever. And I didn't want to send you mixed signals, or make you feel that I didn't want to be with you, because I do. I want to be with you more than anything. I think about it all the time. But there's something bigger behind this. It's one of the reasons I blew up at you at The Met fundraiser.

It's the reason why I protect myself so fiercely. It's something from my past that sometimes creeps into the present."

"You don't have to talk about this."

"Yes, I do."

"Not if you feel unsafe."

"I do feel safe. I need to get this out into the open and just be done with it. When I tell you, you might be finished with me. You might think, 'too much baggage.'"

"I seriously doubt that."

"OK. Well, when I was a kid, my father beat me. He'd get drunk, and he'd take out his anger on me and my mother, who never reported him to the authorities or to child services. I'm not going to go through the laundry list of all that he did to us, but you need to understand that sometimes those memories come flooding back. I have trust issues with men because of it. I still have nightmares about what he did to me, which is another reason I didn't stay the other night. I didn't want to freak you out if I had one."

He studied me for a moment. "I reminded you of your father that night at the Four Seasons, didn't I? You saw something in me that frightened you. That's why you stayed away. I made you think of your father, didn't I?"

"To a degree, yes."

"Jennifer, I'm sorry."

"Alex, this isn't meant to be a guilt trip. It's just so you have a deeper understanding of who I am. I'm twenty-five, and I have zero experience with men beyond my father's abuse. I know you can sense me holding back. I needed you to know that it's not you. It's me."

"No, it isn't." He put his drink beside mine and moved closer to me. "It's him. I'm not going to ask what he did to you. That will come in time, or it won't come at all. It's your choice. The only question I have is whether it was sexual. Because if it was, and if you need additional time to feel like you can trust me before being intimate with me, that's not an issue. When and if it happens, it will just make that moment better."

"None of it was sexual. He just abused me verbally and physically."

"Just?"

"Just. It could have been worse. A lot worse. And to be honest with you, I don't know if I want to wait much longer. Everything in my life is positive right now. I'm in a good space. I'm with a good man.

I know you're a good man. I know that night was a blip. I get it now. And I'm tired of having my father hold me back. He's not going to do so forever. It's time to get on with it."

"It's time to get on with what?"

I just looked at him. My emotions raw and naked. I felt fully exposed and vulnerable at that moment, but also safe with him.

He was looking hard at me. "What's the other reason you wanted to come here tonight, Jennifer?"

"I didn't have a reason until a moment ago."

"What is it?"

It was difficult for me to say the words, but I forced myself to. "I want to be with you. I feel like I've cheated myself by waiting so long. I've lost years because of my hangups. And now here you are, the one man I can see myself with. I think that when we begin, I'm not going to want to stop. Even now it's difficult for me not to touch you. And I want to touch you."

A darkness that was brooding with desire came over his face. His eyes, framed by his thick lashes, narrowed slightly. "Where do you want to touch me?"

"Everywhere," I said.

"You've thought a lot about this, haven't you?"

More than you know. I nodded and felt myself begin to tremble.

"What was the last thought you had?" There was a roughness to his voice that had never been there before. It was intoxicating.

"Touching your chest. Finally seeing it."

"When was this?"

"At work tonight."

"What brought that on?"

I started to feel hot. "You did. I thought of you, and then my mind went there. I want to know every inch of your body. I want to know it better than you do."

He wasn't touching me. He wasn't judging me. He was just listening to me and watching me, but in a way that was different. It was as if he was planning what he was going to do to me. There was a predatory look in his eyes.

"Jennifer, how far do you want to take this?"

"All the way."

"That can be pretty far, and you don't even know how far I'll go. I need to warn you of that, because I will go far. And once I start, it will be a long time before I stop."

"I don't care so long as I feel safe. But I want it to build. I want to be surprised. I want to learn and I don't want you to hold back. If there's something you like to do or that you're into, I want to try it. I want to experience everything."

"Everything?"

"I want you to teach me what you know."

"Are you sure about that?"

"I am."

"That could take some time, you know? And stamina."

"I've got both."

"I can take you to places by barely touching you that will send you out of your body."

"Then do it," I said. "Do it now."

* * *

Upcoming Releases

This story unfolds over the course of multiple novels—not novellas. Each one follows the continuing story of Jennifer Kent and Alexander Wenn. Each book is a full-length novel with substance, not a few Chapters meant to tease you along.

Continue the *Annihilate Me* series when Volume Two hits on July 26, 2013. You can pre-order it on Amazon at: http://amzn.to/112Ov8T.

Look for the third volume in the series on September 20, 2013. You also can pre-order it at: http://amzn.to/11k7rPB.

Please join my mailing list here so you never miss a new book: http://on.fb.me/16T4y1u

Also, join me on Facebook: http://on.fb.me/ZSr29Z. I love to chat with my readers. There, I also do giveaways. I'll see you there soon!

If you would leave a review of this book on Amazon, I'd appreciate it. Reviews are critical to every writer.

About the Author

Christina Ross began writing on nights and weekends while working as an intern for an international, iconic fashion magazine. After eight years, she left that position as an editor. Many of Christina's narratives reflect her background as an insider in the world of fashion.

Now, with a successful fashion career behind her, Christina divides her time between her apartment on Park Avenue in Manhattan and her pied-a-terre on the Ile St. Louis in Paris. Christina enjoys long walks along the Seine, and on Fifth Avenue in New York, where she likes to shop. She also loves spending quality time with her girlfriends in both locations. A lifelong animal-lover, Christina's favorite charity is the ASPCA, to which she encourages all her readers to contribute.

Join Christina on Facebook, where she loves to chat with her readers:https://www.facebook.com/ChristinaRoss.Author